Praise for Melissa Schroeder's
The Spy Who Loved Her

"It is hard to wish for anything other than a happy ending for this perfectly suited pair!"

~ *Romantic Times Magazine*

"Oh, whenever I get a book from Melissa Schroeder in my hand, I know I'm in for a wonderful read and this one proves that she's still an author goddess!"

~ *Love Romances and More*

"*The Spy Who Loved Her* hits many high marks with the romance, dialogue and steamy love scenes. This is one of the better recent historical romances I've read and one I recommend you try."

~ *Katiebabs*

"Captivating story, loved the interaction between Daniel and Anna. Daniel thinks he knows how to handle women, it quickly becomes evident there is one woman who won't be handled. Loved this book."

~ *Sensual Reviews*

"From the moment that Daniel and Anna shared their first waltz, I could not put the book down."

~ *Romance Novel News*

Look for these titles by
Melissa Schroeder

Now Available:

Grace Under Pressure
The Seduction of Widow McEwan
The Last Detail

Harmless
A Little Harmless Sex
A Little Harmless Pleasure
A Little Harmless Obsession
A Little Harmless Lie
A Little Harmless Addiction

Once Upon an Accident
The Accidental Countess
Lessons in Seduction

Print Anthology
Leather and Lace

The Spy Who Loved Her

Melissa Schroeder

SAMHAIN PUBLISHING

Samhain Publishing, Ltd.
11821 Mason Montgomery Road, 4B
Cincinnati, OH 45249
www.samhainpublishing.com

The Spy Who Loved Her
Copyright © 2012 by Melissa Schroeder
Print ISBN: 978-1-60928-410-7
Digital ISBN: 978-1-60928-263-9

Editing by Heidi Moore
Cover by Scott Carpenter

First Samhain Publishing, Ltd. electronic publication: March 2011
First Samhain Publishing, Ltd. print publication: February 2012

Dedication

To Brandy Walker who has always supported me and listened to me gripe. Only other military wives can understand the idiocy we deal with on a regular basis. I truly value your friendship each and every day.

Acknowledgements

No book is ever written without a lot of help. Special thanks for love and support from Kris Cook, Brandy Walker, Ali Flores and Joy Harris. A massive thank you to my Mel's Book Chatters and all of you who continue to support me with each and every book. Always a big thank you to Samhain Publishing for the support they give my writing. And of course, a big, wet, sloppy kiss to Heidi Moore who actually makes the editing process something I enjoy and keeps me on track (even if bright shiny things are so much more fun).

And last, but not least, Les, Audrey, Eliza and Belle. Thank you always for your love and support.

Chapter One

Lady Anna stepped over the threshold to her brother's study and found herself facing a tribunal. Her brother, Sebastian, sat behind his desk. From the irritated look on his face, he was not happy either about what was going to happen, or about having to be the one to do it. Her sister-in-law, Colleen, sat to his right. She offered Anna a reassuring smile that did nothing to reassure her. And then there was her mother, Lady Victoria.

Though she was the mother of two grown children, it was hard to tell. Her face was unlined, her figure trim and womanly. They shared the same cornflower blue eyes and usually an even temper. At the moment, irritation sharpened her usually pleasant features.

"Is there some meeting I had not been told about?" She tried to keep her tone light, but even she heard the thread of fear in her voice and hated herself for it.

No one spoke for a few moments. The ticking clock was the only sound in the room. With each click, the air grew heavier.

"You act as if you are going to gallows," Sebastian said.

She glanced at him. The sun streamed through the window behind his desk showing off the few gray hairs he had acquired in the last several years. Since he'd married, he had become downright stodgy.

"What would you call it?" she asked, crossing her arms

beneath her breasts.

Her mother sniffed. "Please, Anna, sit down so we can have a discussion."

It was not a request. It was a command. Lady Victoria rarely ordered, until recently. She'd turned into a veritable general in the last months.

Anna hesitated, but the hard look from her brother warned her not to buck them on this. With a frustrated sigh, she walked to one of the chairs in front of Sebastian's desk.

"Mother wants you to understand that going to your cousin's ball is not a choice. You must attend."

She had known her mother would insist. Anna was irritated she had yet to come up with a reasonable reason not to go. "I do not know why."

"Why?" Her mother's voice had gone shrill. It was so uncommon that it startled Anna. Lady Victoria was not a woman who yelled, and she definitely didn't argue in the tone of a fishwife.

"Yes. Mother, I understand why most women must go, but I do not. I have no need for a husband."

A strange mixture of pain and sympathy flashed over her mother's face before her features softened. "Anna, darling, you need to stop blaming yourself for what happened."

Just the mention of the events from three years earlier with Dewhurst caused her spine to stiffen. The easy smile Lady Victoria had offered Anna faded. With a resigned air her mother walked to the window.

"You will go tonight," Sebastian again ordered. His voice had hardened, his expression growing colder. This was the brother she had known before Colleen had come into their lives.

Aggravation swept through her and she ground her teeth to keep the frustrated scream from escaping. In recent months, everyone seemed to have an opinion about what she should or should not be doing. They had begged her to attend functions, told her she was wasting her days at the orphanage. This was the first time they had ordered her to go. They acted as if she were the empty-headed twit she used to be.

She wanted nothing more than to tell Sebastian to go bugger himself. The moment that thought popped into her head, she pushed it back to the recesses of her mind. While it might make her feel wonderful for a moment, her brother would not be happy. She shrugged, knowing that now there was no way to avoid his command.

"Anna." Colleen smiled at her. "I know that you would rather do other things."

"Then why are you siding with them?"

"Because I know that this is important. Not going would be a slight to Cicely and Douglas. Finding a husband is not what is important here. Showing your support is."

Anna closed her eyes and willed away the pain. She didn't hate Cicely or Douglas. She loved them both as if they were siblings. Knowing she had almost gotten her cousin killed was sometimes too much to bear. Just thinking about Cicely made her heart ache. Seeing her reminded Anna of her folly. It physically hurt to be in the same room.

Anna opened her eyes and studied her brother. She knew he did this out of love, and Colleen had been correct.

"I will attend."

She said nothing as she walked to the door. The sharp jab of betrayal she had felt earlier could not compete with the fear now fluttering in her chest. She was not prepared to be in the presence of her cousin.

"Anna," her mother called out.

Anna did not turn around. She was not able to. For a moment, she wasn't sure if her mother would say anything, then she said, "Please dress accordingly."

Anna slipped out the door and closed it behind her. She noticed Templeton standing beside the door and frowned at him. "You knew what they were about."

The impassive servant frowned back. "I work for your brother, my lady."

"It would not hurt to warn me."

"I believe if I had, you would have found something else to do, and that would not have pleased your brother."

With a huff, she headed to the stairs. Templeton knew her better than most of her acquaintances. She had been a mischievous girl and had many adventures. Some of which would have landed her in trouble had she not had Templeton's help. There were many times he had outright lied to Sebastian. It was another layer of betrayal that he seemed to be in the enemy camp.

She entered her room and found her maid, Dory, readying a bath.

"*Et tu*, Dory?"

The young woman stared at her, her blue eyes rounded. "*Et* what?"

Anna shook her head. "You knew what they were up to and you allowed me to go?"

Dory rushed forward, worry etched on her facial features. "Oh, no, my lady. It was after you left that Mrs. Flowers told me to get a bath ready."

She said nothing as she walked to her window to look out upon the day. Everything on the busy street looked normal, somehow in the right order of things. No one looking at her would know the turmoil that tumbled through her. The sounds of Dory readying her bath faded into the background as she mentally prepared herself for the evening ahead. People knew she did not go out in public unless she was looking for funds for the orphanage. But those were usually smaller gatherings, without the need to explain why she was there. Yes, the fact she was related to the Duke and Duchess was reason enough, but that would not discourage the fortune hunters. She would be fending off advances all night long.

"My lady," Dory said, her voice tentative.

Anna looked over her shoulder at her.

"Your bath is ready."

She nodded then looked back out the window.

"Don't let it get cold."

"I won't," she promised, but did not look around. She did not have the patience to be nice to anyone. The moment she heard the door click shut, she sighed and stepped away from the window. Alone, with only the faint sounds from the street below, Anna allowed her shoulders to slump and take in the betrayal she felt. She knew her mother and Sebastian meant well. They would never do anything to hurt her...not purposely. She needed to be reminded of her duty, that was true. But there was a tiny part of her that yearned to defy them.

She had paid her penance these last three years. She had dedicated herself to good works and the broadening of her mind. At first, her family had seemed happy with her choice in activities. The trips to the lending library paired with her charity work had even earned her respect with some of the matrons of society. For the first time in her life, Anna had felt...useful. When she discovered St. Mark's orphanage, she knew she had found her calling. But as she found peace in her work with children, her mother had grown restless. Anna did not know what had prompted her mother, but she had slowly turned from the understanding mother Anna had known her life, to a formidable foe. She had been able to ignore her mother's requests and orders, until Sebastian had added his voice to them. Now the only feeling she had was that of being trapped.

If she were truthful with herself, she was angrier at herself.

She was in this situation because of her behavior with Dewhurst. She had made a total fool of herself over a man who should not have been trusted. Still, she was happy for her cousin. Cicely had found true love with Douglas. What she could not understand was why her family could not be happy for her.

Forcing her mind away from her morose thoughts, she moved toward the bath. There was no fighting over what would happen tonight. She would make the best of it and possibly gather up some more money for the orphanage. Before she could disrobe, a knock sounded at the door. Colleen did not wait for an invitation and poked her head through the opening.

"Are you all right?" Concern filled her expression.

She offered her sister-in-law a wry smile. "For being bullied and manhandled, I seem to be holding up."

Colleen grimaced, slipped through the doorway and shut it behind her. "I was not completely in agreement with their tactics."

"But their purpose?"

"Anna, you cannot go about as you have. And this ball is important. Not going is a slight to your cousin and mine."

Colleen's cousin was the Duke of Ethingham, Cicely's husband. "I don't think that I would be missed."

Colleen let one eyebrow rise.

"Oh, all right, I understand that some will think it a slight, but both of our cousins will understand. More than likely, they will not want me there."

"What nonsense."

"It is true."

Colleen shook her head. "They both think that you are coming."

"Only due to the fact that Sebastian said I would."

"You cannot think they would not want you there. That is absurd."

Panic, irritation and fear entwined a tight fist around her heart. Before she could stop herself, her cloistered feelings spilled out. "Think, Colleen. Would you want the person who helped a madman abduct your love? Why everyone does not understand is beyond my comprehension."

The outburst happened so quickly that the silence that followed stunned Anna. For a moment, Colleen said nothing. Then pity filled her expression. Embarrassment and shame shifted through Anna and she had to turn away. She rarely talked about her feelings on the subject.

"Anna?" Colleen's voice was gentle. "You should not blame yourself. Cicely and Douglas do not blame you."

Anna swallowed the lump that had formed in her throat. "They should."

She could feel the burning of tears against the backs of her eyes as she tried to hold onto her composure. "I do not understand why they even want to see me there. And I have much to do at St. Mark's."

Colleen said nothing. Anna glanced over her shoulder at her.

"Dear heart, you are not responsible for what Dewhurst did." Anna opened her mouth to argue but Colleen raised her hand. "But I do understand that while the rest of us do not fault you, you do. How much longer will you blame yourself for the actions of a devious man?"

Anna blinked, but the tears fell. "I do not know if I can."

Colleen pulled her into her arms briefly. "You must, Anna, or you will never be happy. That is all we want."

"I understand that, but I do not know if I am ready." *If I will ever be ready.*

Colleen pulled back and smiled at her. "You will. You just

13

need to open your mind to it. Now, young lady, please do get dressed and for goodness' sake wear something bright. Your mother will have an apoplexy if you wear something gray."

She thought back to her mother's behavior. Lady Victoria was usually a bit more subtle in her ministrations. In the past few weeks, she had become more and more adamant and well...pushy. "Is something bothering Mother?"

"She has a daughter who will not go to a social event unless it is tied to good works."

Anna shook her head. "No. Have you noticed that she has been a bit...well, shrill lately."

Her face softened into an understanding smile. "Your mother loves you. Since you are hurting, she is hurting. It is a motherly thing, dear. I will leave you to your bath."

Moments later, Anna slipped into the heated, fragrant water. It eased her muscles but not her mind...or her heart. She wanted to be a good daughter. Anna had thought she had succeeded—until recently. When she was a frivolous debutant, she never gave a passing thought to the poor, or just how people suffered. It shamed her to admit, but it was true. She would have never thought people would criticize her choices now. She had promised her mother and Sebastian she would go, and she would keep that promise. But that did not mean she had to stay all night. As she slipped further into the warm water, Anna calculated just how long she had to stay at the ball to satisfy her mother.

The rustle of silk was the first thing Daniel heard as he slowly returned to consciousness. Since he was in his family townhouse, he knew without a doubt it wasn't anyone but the one person he wanted to avoid today.

"Mother?"

"It is almost four in the afternoon."

Her voice told him that he had breached some rule she had put in place. Lately, she had been getting overly concerned with his comings and goings.

"Yes, and being that I got in this morning just as the sun was coming up, I definitely am not ready to get up."

Another rustle of silk, then a wave of flowery perfume. It was at that moment, he remembered he wasn't wearing a stitch of clothing. He scrambled, turning over and grabbing his bed linens. He pulled them up to his chest. The fast actions left his body throbbing in pain.

"Really, Daniel. It is not as if I have not seen you naked before." Humor threaded her voice.

He grimaced as he rose to sit against his headboard. His ribs were still sore from the fight last night.

"Oh, darling boy, what have you done to yourself?" The concern in her voice was genuine, and as he watched her settle on the bed next to him, he could see it there plain in her gaze. For all her faults, his mother truly loved all her children.

"I did nothing to myself." He pulled himself to sit against the pillows against his headboard. "But a nasty Russian caught us unawares last night. I think he bruised my ribs."

She frowned. "You are getting too old for this."

He chuckled. "I am just over thirty. Father was working well into his fifties."

She sighed. "First, your father still worked for the state department. He did not go out running around picking fights with Russian spies. Secondly, your father had already married by that point and we had started a family."

He groaned. "Please, not this again, Mother."

"I thought once Sebastian was married you would follow suit."

His usual response to these discussions was to leave. The problem was that she had him trapped. That was, unless he wanted to traipse around nude in front of her. Even he wasn't brave enough to do that. And from the shrewd look in her hazel eyes, she knew she had him.

"I have told you that I will not marry until there is someone to take my place."

"Hmph. That is not going to happen if you do not marry and set up a nursery. Unless..."

Her gaze grew unfocused as something bubbled in her dangerous mind. His father said he had never known a man who could out plot his mother.

"What about your cousin? Simon was being trained by your uncle...well, before. He is five and twenty, definitely old enough to handle overseeing things while you do this."

He should have known she would latch onto Simon. "His father died less than six months ago."

She nodded acknowledging his comment. A flash of pain came and went so fast most would have missed it. Harold had actually been his father's uncle, but they had been as close as if they were brothers. His death was still raw for the entire family.

"Have you been able to find who poisoned him?"

He shook his head. "No. Joanna seems to have a lead on a Russian, but that is it. She can barely go out into society, and most see her as a pariah."

His mother smiled. "And knowing Jo, she enjoys that. She was never one for ball and musicales."

"My only worry is that she is becoming obsessed with finding the spy. Being cut off from society has allowed her to turn all her attention to the task."

Her smile faded. "I will talk to her. She still blames herself for it."

He nodded but said nothing.

"You will attend the Ethinghams' ball tonight."

He wanted to groan but knew better not to. He might be a man and an earl, but she was his mother. Lady Adelaide would not hesitate to box his ears if he refused her demand. And, dammit to all, he was in too much pain to deal with that tonight. Trussing up in his evening clothes was going to be painful enough as it was.

"I don't know if Sebastian would forgive you if you missed it."

Sebastian didn't care if he showed up or not, but apparently his mother did.

"Is there a particular reason?"

She sighed. "Lady Victoria asked."

And that sealed it. With Sebastian's mother pairing up with his, there was no way to win.

"I understand my duties, Mother."

She brushed a lock of hair away from his forehead. "Even when you were a little boy you did." She cupped his cheek, a familiar move she had used when he was a lad. "Just know that filling your father's shoes is not everything there is in life, dear boy. You need some outside activities."

"I do other things."

She dropped her hand. "I am not talking about your mistresses or paramours."

Heat filled his face. He should be accustomed to his mother's plain talk, but he did not know a man who was. There was something so...wrong, discussing your love life with your mother—especially while naked.

"I am talking about the future. Take time to make one for yourself."

He nodded as she leaned forward and kissed his forehead.

As she walked toward the door, she said, "And you will accompany me to the ball. No escaping to your club."

He chuckled as he threw off his bed covers. He pulled on his robe and tied the sash. A knock sounded at the door.

"Come."

His valet opened the door and stepped inside.

"Really, my lord. These late nights are not good for you."

He chuckled. "Are you telling me that I am past my salad days?"

"Oh, you passed those days years ago. Now it is getting embarrassing."

Daniel frowned. "Embarrassing?"

"Roving all over kingdom come, for what? Spy games? It is well past time you set up a nursery."

Daniel groaned. "Not you too."

"I see that your mother has talked to you about it."

"It is her favorite subject of discussion. You would think she would busy herself with my sisters."

"With Lady Portia married, she is content for now with your sisters."

"But not with me."

Jenkins opened his mouth, but Daniel lifted a hand. "No more. It is bad enough I have to rearrange a meeting meant for tonight for later this week. I have agreed to go to the ball. Leave it be."

With a sniff, Jenkins moved to his wardrobe and seemingly got down to work. It figured his mother would enlist Jenkins in her plot. He had been with them for years and knew much about the Bridgertons...being a former spy himself. And knowing his mother, she had convinced Jenkins that it was imperative he do everything he could to make sure Daniel did his duty.

His mother knew him better than anyone should. The two of them had weathered some very tough storms together. When his father had been murdered, Daniel had only been thirteen. His mother had married young, and at the age of one and thirty found herself a widow with a horde of children to raise and spy ring to run. Not your average life.

As the bath water was being brought up and poured into the tub, Daniel looked out upon Mayfair. He knew his mother wanted him to marry, and for that reason he had not told her of his decision. Marriage and children was something he would never have. He could not do what he needed to do and have a life outside of that. His mother was the strongest woman he knew and the loss of her husband had almost killed her. Watching her struggle had a profound effect on him. He had promised himself he would never marry.

A man who lived life waiting to see who wanted to kill him next could not have that luxury.

Chapter Two

"Do smile, Anna. It cannot be all that dire."

She glanced up at her cousin by marriage as he twirled her around the dance floor. From the moment she'd arrived both cousins had ensured she felt comfortable, and Douglas had even insisted on a waltz with her. It was the only dance she had accepted, even with the warning looks her mother kept tossing her way.

"You cannot complain, my lord. This is your ball. There was a time you avoided these activities as if it were the plague. Now you are having one in your own home."

Douglas smiled. "Yes, but it makes my wife happy. I am ever ready to do that." He glanced at his wife who was presently dancing with an earl. "Even if I have to share her with everyone else."

The disgruntled expression on his face made her laugh. It was a joy to see a man who loved his wife so much. Especially Cicely. No one deserved loving attention more than her cousin. "I daresay she could care less about everyone else."

His cheeks reddened and she laughed again.

"Oh, my. I made you blush."

He cleared his throat and looked over her shoulder. "What I want to know is why you have refused so many dances, but you accepted mine?"

"You are family."

He cocked his head and brought his gaze back to meet hers. "I have been warned by your mother not to discuss this, but I truly wish you would not allow what happened to affect you in this way."

Her face flamed and she looked around. Sebastian, and not to mention Douglas, had made sure that not a whiff of scandal touched her. Still, she could not help the feeling that people knew. She swallowed a lump in her throat that threatened to choke her. She concentrated on his chest. "I thank you for your understanding."

"Anna." His voice was stern and not like the Douglas she knew. It was the one Cicely hated the most...his ducal voice. She forced herself to meet his gaze.

"I do not want you to waste your life because you feel you are responsible for what happened."

"Working with orphans is wasting my life?"

He studied her for a moment. "No. That is a worthy cause. But caring for another woman's child is not the same as having one of your own."

Pain and irritation entwined as it thrummed through her blood. She knew he felt he had the right to comment, but it was going too far. Some of what she was thinking must have shown in her face.

"I do apologize for being so forward, but I do not want you to suffer because of that mess. You were not at fault any more than Cicely was."

She nodded.

He smiled. "Now, I wanted to tell you that we expect another bundle of joy to be presented to us in several months."

And with that, he whirled her away and Anna forced herself to concentrate.

"What are you doing here on the sidelines?" Daniel asked his best friend. "You are usually out on the floor with your wife."

Sebastian smiled as he glanced in the direction of Colleen who was sitting between both of their mothers. "She is feeling a little under the weather at the moment."

"Nothing serious."

A small smile curved Sebastian's lips. "No. She will be fine."

"Your sister looks as if she hates every minute of that waltz," Daniel said as he watched the duke expertly steer her around the floor.

Sebastian grimaced. "She is not presenting herself very well tonight, is she?"

Daniel could not disagree with that. Anyone who knew Anna could tell from the set of her shoulders that she was not happy with the circumstances. She often pulled her shoulders back when she was irritated. And the smile she offered the duke was not one of genuine smiles. This one curved her lips but did not meet her eyes. There had been a time when every smile showed the exuberant joy she felt inside. Those smiles were a rare occurrence these days.

"Daniel?"

He shook himself free of the thoughts. "You know she didn't want to be here. She is doing her duty. It is all you can expect."

Sebastian grunted. "I thought if she were to attend—"

"You got it in your head she would find a man and fall madly in love? How many of these soirees have you taken her to in the last few months?"

"I just don't want her wasting her time working at that orphanage. She could have her pick of men, but she pays them no heed."

True to Sebastian's comments, the waltz ended and

Douglas walked her back to her mother. As he did, men's heads turned, watching. The available gentlemen followed. They surrounded her, each trying to gain her attention, but she barely noticed. If he didn't know better, he would think she would rather meet the guillotine than speak to one of them.

"You need to ask her to dance. A waltz."

His heart leapt at the idea of holding Anna in his arms, touching her. It would be heaven and hell combined.

"No."

He said it loud enough for a few people to turn to Daniel and stare at him as if he had grown horns in his head.

"Excuse me?"

He opened his mouth, but then closed it again. He had avoided this situation for years. The one waltz he had shared with her the first year she had been out had been painful. The moment she had stepped into his arms, his body had reacted. For the first time since his youth, he found his palms sweating and his mind completely blank. The lust encased in a thick layer of guilt had been enough to cause any man to go mad.

He glanced at Sebastian who continued to watch his sister with a frown. How did one tell his best friend he was lusting after his younger sister? It was a rule that you did not even think of your friend's sister that way. You just did not do it.

Sebastian turned his attention back to Daniel. "If you do not dance with her, people will wonder. Douglas is family and she dances with no one else?"

"He is the host. Besides, it will probably make her that much more popular."

Not that she needed help in that quarter. With her soft blue eyes, perfect skin and petite, rounded body, most men drew to her. There was a way she looked at a man, focusing her entire attention on him, that made most lose their heads. He knew. He had been given that sort of attention one time, long ago. It was one of the reasons he had to stay away from her. Very far away.

"There will be talk. I know you understand."

Daniel knew what he meant. Douglas had had a reputation for being a rake of the first order before meeting Cicely, and gossip, no matter how far from the truth, could wound.

"Please, Daniel."

Daniel felt the hatchet lower. Sebastian did not ask much of him, and he rarely said please. Daniel shot him a look and wanted nothing more than to smack the self-satisfied smile curving his friend's lips.

"You owe me a boon."

Sebastian nodded. "I agree."

Without a backward glance, he started on his trek across the ballroom to where Anna was holding court.

"Daniel?"

He turned and found his father's best friend and his honorary uncle, Lord Elwood, waving a finger in the air. Knowing his duty, Daniel changed direction and moved to make his way to the older man.

"I am surprised to find you here tonight," he remarked as he grabbed a glass of champagne from a passing footman. Lord Horace Elwood had been his father's friend since Eton. As Horace always told it, his father had stepped in to protect him during a fight and they had been friends from that moment on. His hair was no longer the sandy brown of his youth, but now laced with gray and thinning on top. He had become a permanent part of their lives from the moment his father had died. In a house surrounded by women, Daniel had always been thankful for the friendship offered by Horace.

"Mother."

Horace's blue eyes danced over his glass as he sipped. "Oh, I understand now. Anxious for you to set up a nursery, is she?"

Daniel nodded as he glanced in Anna's direction. "Did she tell you about it?"

He chuckled. "I would not admit it if she did. But it is normal for your mother to want you to settle."

Lord Smythe made a move to step closer to Anna, causing Daniel to frown. The way she was smiling up at the man there was bound to be talk. She should know better than to even give the man any attention. Bloody hell, she had to know his reputation.

"Ah, I see you have your eye on someone already."

Daniel glanced at him. "I do?"

He gestured in the direction of Anna with his glass. "It is understandable. With her fortune and good looks, she is a catch. Her do-gooder status is a trouble."

He shook his head trying to keep track of Horace's conversation. "Trouble?"

"Well, my dear boy, you cannot have a wife around that sort of riff raff. Very unseemly."

Daniel nodded again, not wanting to get into another argument with him. The one fault that Horace possessed was a bone-deep snobbishness.

"Either way, I am doing this as a favor to Sebastian and I better make my way over there before the next waltz."

"Happy hunting, my dear boy."

Daniel fought the need to groan at the image of him hunting for a wife and started on his path again. With each step, his heart sped up, his body reacted. It had been like this since she had come to town several years earlier. He, a man who had been with countless women, who was renowned for his seduction skills, found himself at a loss of what to do when in the presence of Anna. That was, until three years ago. Since then she had avoided soirees of this type. Lately though, it had been easier. She had become more conservative in her dress.

Unfortunately, tonight Daniel detected her mother's hand in her choice of outfits.

The delicate blue silk draped her curves, making the most of her small waist. It showed entirely too much of her breasts in Daniel's opinion. Indeed, Lord Smythe was practically drooling as he talked to her bosom. Possessive anger whipped through him as his blood heated and he clenched his fists. Damn her mother for putting her on display like a prize to be won.

Knowing that it would be better to get the deed done, Daniel approached her. He elbowed his way through the sea of young men surrounding his quarry. The moment he stepped up next to her, he found himself unable to speak. Anna was responding to a question from some wet-behind-the-ears viscount and not even looking at him. But even so, his palms began to sweat. When she turned to him, he felt the blood drain from his head. Those huge blue eyes always did it to him. No matter how many times he reminded himself he could not lust after Sebastian's sister, his body ignored him. When she met his gaze, every warning he gave himself dissolved.

"Lord Bridgerton." Her voice had dipped an octave as it slipped over his nerve endings. Cultured English draped in a layer of sensuality. "I did not expect to see you in attendance."

He knew he should throw out a witty rejoinder, but his brain refused to work. It had been months since he had seen her dressed for a ball. The impact of her appearance singed across his senses. Even standing several feet away from her, he could catch wisps of her fragrance. Rose water. He could never smell it and not think of her or imagine spending a night searching out the scent on her flesh.

Just thinking it brought images to mind, causing his cock to harden. Christ, he had not had this problem in public since...well, the last time he danced with her.

"Lord Bridgerton?"

It took him a moment to detect the worry in her voice. It

was enough to snap his mind away from his lust-filled thoughts.

"Lady Anna." He bowed. "I have come to beg a dance with you."

The first strains of the next waltz filtered over the crowd. From the look on her face he could tell she knew he had timed it on purpose.

Before she could respond, Lord Smythe decided to speak for her. "Lady Anna is not dancing tonight."

The look she shot the idiot would have shriveled any man's parts, but Lord Smythe was not paying attention. She opened her mouth to blast the earl, but Daniel decided to stop her from verbally smashing the man. He did not have time to listen to the pup make a fool of himself.

He gave the young viscount a measured look. "Ah, but Lady Anna is considered a close family friend. Indeed, her mother and mine are bosom pals."

"Indeed, Lord Bridgerton. I would be happy to share this dance."

Her cool tone caught his attention. When he looked at her, he saw a look in her eyes that told him she knew Sebastian had ordered him over there.

"You honor me."

He took her hand and rested it on his as he guided them through the crowd. She said nothing as he pulled her into his arms and whisked her into the waltz.

Anna ordered her heart to stop beating so hard. Surely everyone could hear even over the musicians. She had known the moment Daniel had come upon her group. She had done everything to calm herself down, but nothing seemed to work. It was an embarrassing situation. The one man she seemed to be interested in was the one man she could not stand.

"No comment for me, My Lady Poppet?"

Oh, she hated that name. It had been his name for her from the moment Sebastian had brought him home one day on break from Eton. She had loved it at first. What girl would not? Daniel was a charming man, graced with a type of Adonis beauty that belied his true personality. His brown hair had been a bit overgrown and his golden eyes had always been kind.

When she had come to town, she had been so sure he would treat her with the proper respect. It was her fault she allowed her girlish dreams to build a fantasy that would never come true. She had expected her playmate, a man who could always make her smile no matter how horrible of a day she had. Instead, he had been distant and they had slipped into a strange sort of argumentative friendship. They could rarely be in each other's presence without a fight ensuing. The truth had crushed her usually exuberant spirit. He thought of her as nothing but a poppet, a child, and always would.

No matter how many times she told herself to ignore him, she could not stop the way her body reacted. It was most unsettling. Still, she would not back down, because he would know that he had gotten to her. She willed herself to look into his eyes and knew the moment their gazes locked, it had been a mistake. Heat flared low in her tummy, feathering out over her body.

Oh, bother.

To save herself from embarrassment, she focused on a point over his shoulder.

"I know you are doing this for Sebastian."

"Indeed?"

Even without seeing his expression, she knew he had raised one eyebrow. The condescension was easy to hear. But she would know even without that. She knew everything about him. His moods, his expressions, his faults, and even knowing all of that, she still loved him. Or had. Her fantasy had been shattered when she had made it to town. Then she had realized that the façade she had believed in never truly existed. But that was just one of many fumbles she had made in her first years in town.

She brushed her thoughts aside and concentrated on finishing the dance.

"Your brother is worried."

Of course, how could she forget? He would never ask her to dance if her brother had not asked him to.

She huffed out a sigh. "He has become a worrywart."

Daniel laughed. It was a sound she did not hear often anymore and even as she cursed it, her heart warmed at the sound. "Yes. I will say from the moment he married, your brother changed."

She glanced up at him sharply, studying his features. "But for the better."

He looked down at her and the breath tangled in her throat. She could not help it. His pretty looks were renowned in the ton. She had known even before coming to town that women were drawn to him. Thick light brown hair, those dark golden brown eyes with thick, dark lashes, not to mention his calculating wit and solid physique, attracted most women. Unfortunately, she had been one of those women and it did not seem she had freed herself of the affliction.

"Agreed. I would never have thought it, but Sebastian definitely flourishes in the realm of married life."

"I assumed that is why you were made to dance attendance tonight."

He frowned. "What do you mean?"

"I understood from my mother that your mother wants you to settle down."

He grimaced and she laughed. Her brother had worn that

29

look more than once before meeting Colleen.

"Yes. My mother rang peal over me again claiming I am a doddering old fool who must marry."

"The problem would be finding a woman who would marry you."

He smiled and she tried to ignore the way her heart skipped.

"True. But my mother assures me there is any number of young ladies who would be interested."

Her heart squeezed at the thought of him marrying some debutant. She knew it would come to this one day. He would have to marry, being the only son. But still, there was a twinge of pain when she thought of him marrying some faceless, brainless debutant.

"Ow."

She realized she was squeezing his hand. "Do forgive me."

"I am assuming you are here for the same reason?"

She snorted at the suggestion. "I think not. Mother thought it important that I attend, being family. Apparently, Cicely still worries about being accepted within certain circles."

"I daresay she will never have a problem, especially with the title of duchess and after providing the duke with an heir."

Anna nodded and glanced fleetingly at her cousin. Three years earlier, the radiant beauty had been a wallflower more comfortable with her books than people. Falling in love with Douglas had changed that, although she was the same sweet woman.

"We know that, but Cicely does not. You understand."

He did of course because Daniel was as close as family, closer in a lot of ways that most of the ton did not know. He knew the rumors about Cicely, knew the truth of them. She knew there was not much her brother did not share with him.

"Your mother used that to get you out tonight?"

She made a face. "Partially, because she knows I would do anything to help my cousins. She also thinks that my choice in activities is not good."

"I have to disagree."

That surprised her and some of what she thought must have shown on her face.

"Why do you look so astonished?"

"You disagree with my mother?"

He inclined his head. "While I am not sure exactly what they are, your brother said something about the orphanage? You enjoy it. You do good work knowing you. I have to admire that."

A warm glow of excitement rolled through her. Most of the men of their class thought of her activity as a waste of time. Only her brother and sister-in-law seemed to think it a worthy cause.

"Still, I can also understand your mother wanting you to get married. Can you not continue your activities and be married?"

She shook her head. "Some men might not have a problem with it. That is not what holds me back. I decided three years ago that I would not marry. It isn't for me."

The music ended. They stopped dancing but Daniel did not release her. The world fell away, the chattering debutants, the clink of glasses, even the people who stepped around them to leave the dance floor. Heat gathered in her tummy as she stared up into his eyes. Something changed, darkened the gold. She felt the need to move away from that look, from her own need to believe in it, but at the same time, she wanted to step closer, feel his arms wrap around her, pulling her against his body. Every bit of moisture dried up in her mouth as her breasts grew heavy. He stepped closer, leaning his head closer to hers.

"The music is done, Bridgerton. Move along."

Lord Smythe's nasty voice sliced through the spell they both seemed to have fallen under. Daniel dropped her hand and stepped away. The look he shot Smythe probably would have made most men run away in terror...and Smythe practically did that as he scurried off the floor with his dance partner. Daniel drew in a deep breath and offered her his arm. Tentatively, she placed her hand on it. Daniel easily guided her through the crowd back to their mothers and the gaggle of men who seemed destined to irritate her. Daniel bowed over her hand.

"Thank you for the dance, Lady Anna," he said, his voice deepening on her name. Wet heat slid through her.

She nodded but could say nothing. Her mind was still spinning, her body yearning to be near him again. He turned quickly, but not before she saw him give both their mothers an almost imperceptible nod.

A sharp shard of pain pricked her heart. She had known that he had been doing it as a favor to her brother, but seeing him acknowledge it in front of her was humiliating. No one else seemed to notice as the conversation flowed around her. She smiled and pretended to listen to the men. But really, how could she pay attention to men who talked more of themselves than anyone or anything else. Surreptitiously, she watched Daniel as he made his way through the crowd, smiling and greeting acquaintances.

"I do believe you will have a bang up time," Viscount Addison said.

It took her a moment to realize he was talking to her. "Excuse me?"

"The house party my father is having. Your mother said you would be happy to attend."

It took every bit of her control not to scream, but anger swept through her. Her mother knew she particularly was not interested in Viscount Addison. He was but three and twenty, one year older than she.

But as she turned to cut her mother a look, she saw Daniel in a heated discussion with Lady Joanna. Odd, since the lady in question was still in mourning. But the woman had never worried about society dictates.

"Seems that Bridgerton is having problems with his new lady love," Lord Greenwood said.

She looked at him, showing him her displeasure. But before she could tell him just how much he'd irritated her, Addison said, "Greenwood, really. There is a lady present."

Greenwood flushed. "I beg your pardon."

She nodded.

"I say, Lady Anna, would you care to take in some fresh air?" Addison asked.

Thankful for what he had done, and not the least bit worried about him, she accepted.

But as they walked toward the French doors, she watched Daniel slip out the ballroom doors with Lady Joanna.

Chapter Three

"Are you positive of the name?" Daniel asked, his mind turning over the news Jo had dropped in his lap.

She nodded and settled back against the seat of the carriage. "Jack ferreted it out. Duchovny, from two sources. And you know his leads are always right."

As he mulled over the information she had just given him, he studied his aunt by marriage. The tell-tale flush of excitement brightened her face. These last few months she had been more than a little preoccupied with finding her husband's killer. Now that she apparently had a name, she would become impossible to deal with.

"I don't want you going after this man. Not until we know for sure."

"I do not work for you."

Her tone was sharp, her eyes narrowed. Daniel knew she felt she failed her husband. But truthfully, if he hadn't seen it coming, no one could have. He was one of the best in the business.

"I understand your frustration, but do not go overboard. We cannot have you exposed."

She said nothing as she turned to look out the window.

"Jo."

She snuck a look at him. "I agree. And the man isn't here."

"Where is he?"

"The Americas from what we gather. There is talk he is due back here later this year."

"You cannot kill him when we find him."

One sculpted eyebrow rose. "Indeed?"

"Not until we know who hired him."

She cast her eyes heavenward. "You act as if I have never run an operation. Your uncle trained me well."

"Then once we know, we decide what to do with him."

She crossed her arms and said nothing.

"Joanna, it is my right as his nephew."

"Great-nephew. And I think that I have more of a right as his widow."

He heard the pain, knew she still mourned her husband. Society had painted her as a cold woman, one who took her nephew as a lover within days of her husband's death. Nothing could be further from the truth.

True, forty years had separated his uncle and aunt, but they'd had an admiration for one another. He had seen them together, had witnessed their glances, their ability to finish each other's sentences. The day of his uncle's death was a blur, all for one defining memory. The stoic Lady Joanna, a woman who rarely showed much emotion, had collapsed into heart-wrenching sobs. It was the only time he had seen her so vulnerable. For that alone, he would happily hunt down his murderer and make him cry before he killed the bastard.

"Let's decide that when we find him."

She hesitated, then nodded.

With nothing else to discuss, he settled his head against the back of his seat. He was tired and sore. That Russian had beat the living hell out of him. He hated to admit it, but the ball had given him a reason to retire early, thanks to Joanna arriving with her news.

"She's very beautiful."

He didn't open his eyes. "Who?"

"Lady Anna."

The amusement in her voice forced him to crack his eyes open. He could see her smirk even in the dim carriage.

"I think most people would agree with you."

She chuckled. "But I think you in particular."

Uncomfortable with the subject at hand, he feigned indifference and looked out the window. It was dark, she could not really see him, but Jo had an intuition about these types of things. One that he was in no mood to discuss.

"What do you mean?"

"Oh, Daniel, it is obvious."

Mortification filled him as he sat straighter. The only way to fight this was to ignore her comment. "Do you have any idea where this poisoner is?"

"America. I told you that."

"Where in America?"

She shrugged. "We are not really sure where, although Jack thinks he might be on the eastern coast."

She smiled, one that filled her face and reminded him just why his uncle had married her. She was an incomparable beauty. Not that she was much prettier than most other women, but there was something so striking about her. Dark raven hair, brown eyes and a skin tone that made you think of foreign lands. She turned heads wherever she went. She stunned a man with her beauty while gaining his secrets. It was her specialty.

"I see Lady Anna a lot down in the White Chapel area."

That had his complete attention. "What do you mean?"

"She comes to that foundling home to work. I am sure you

have heard her talk about it."

"But no decent woman would be seen down there." The moment he said it, he realized his faux pas. Joanna had grown up in the area and frequently visited family and friends down there. His face heated.

"Oh, stop looking so embarrassed. I know what you mean. But Lady Anna is...different."

"By going into one of the worst slums of London? I cannot think what Sebastian is thinking letting her wander around there." In fact, he was surprised Sebastian did not order her away from the area. Anna had been right. Sebastian had gotten a bit overprotective in the last few years.

"Oh, stop being so pompous. You sound like Simon."

Normally, being compared to his arrogant younger cousin would upset him, but he paid no attention to her comment. "No wonder her mother is beside herself. What can the chit be thinking?"

"She is no longer a young girl. I think she is old enough to make her own decisions. She is definitely more mature than she was just a few years ago. Besides, I actually find it admirable."

That caught his attention. "What do you mean?"

"Most women of her class would show up at the holidays, hand out some gifts or give money. Lady Anna is committed to those children. She is known throughout the neighborhood. She even helps working girls find a better way of life."

The image of Anna surrounded by a horde of pox-ridden whores sent a shiver of ice through his blood. Good God! Her mother had every right to worry about what she was doing.

"Oh, I can see it on your face you disapprove. But it is my understanding that she has come into her fortune and there is not much any man can do to stop her."

"That is utterly ridiculous." He crossed his arms over his chest.

"What?"

"Allowing women of her class to go running around in control of their money."

Jo sniffed. "I do just fine."

"Yes, well, you have a background to help you, and Harold taught you how to handle money. Anna is not the type of woman that would be able to handle such things."

The carriage came to a stop in front of her townhouse. For a moment she said nothing. "I think that you have some misconceptions about Lady Anna. She is truly not the girl you knew, and she is definitely not the woman you knew three years ago."

"I have known the chit since she was in the schoolroom. There isn't much I don't know about her."

Including that she still held a *tendre* for the man who had attempted to seduce her and plotted to kill her cousin. He had not known for sure before he had looked in her eyes tonight. He heard it in her voice, knew that she thought it impossible to love again. She had still not let go of the man she had thought the scoundrel to be. It was no wonder she was not looking for a husband for she was still holding onto a memory.

Jo patted him on the knee much as his mother would. It was odd because she was two years his junior, but she seemed wise beyond her years. Her life before and after her marriage to his uncle had given her that. He still did not know if she would ever be able to move on until they found his killer.

"I will let you know what else Jack finds out about our Russian."

He studied her for a moment. Even in the dim light he saw the dark circles beneath her eyes, the weariness in her expression. "He was lucky to have you for a wife, Jo."

She smiled, but this time it was tinged with sadness. "Not lucky enough."

Before he could say another word, she was stepping down from the carriage and was swept into the townhouse. In the past six months, he had yet to convince her that she had not been at fault for her husband's death. Everything in her life was now centered on one thing, finding the man who killed Harold. His real worry now was that it was clouding her judgment. It could make her sloppy. Sloppy spies ended up dead.

The carriage rumbled down the street, taking him back to his townhouse. One thing he knew, Jo had good information. She had some of the best informants. If they said a man named Duchovny killed Harold, it was a safe bet to say the information was right. It had taken six months to get the name of the poisoner, which told him that the man had a well-placed benefactor. It was something that both he and Jo had thought from the beginning. He would have to contact some of his friends in the War Department to see what they had heard, who might be in need of money.

But as soon as he finished making his plans for the next day, Jo's comments about Anna came back to mind. What did Sebastian think he was doing allowing her to run amuck through White Chapel? He understood she wanted to help, but why did she think she needed to be down there? People didn't expect it. Of course, knowing Anna, she would go the unusual route. She always did.

He made a mental note to call on Sebastian the next day. He knew Sebastian understood some of what went on down in those areas, but Daniel had spent much of the last few years down there. He understood the horrible fate many women suffered.

There was one thing for sure. He would do everything in his power to make sure that Sebastian kept her safely tucked away in Mayfair.

With that thought, he settled back on the seat to have a bit of a nap before returning home.

"Do you understand what you must do?"

The ruffian nodded as he downed another tankard of ale. "You want me to knife the man. No problem."

"You know where to find him. Be fast about it and get out of the area."

Without another word, the lord stood and walked toward the door of the pub. No one would recognize him, although it was dangerous. There was always some member of the ton down in this part of White Chapel to enjoy the seamier joys of town life. He stepped outside, ignored the men arguing while a whore called out to him. He stepped up into the handsome cab and found Atterly, his man of business, waiting for him.

"I trust all went well, my lord."

"Yes. I hired a man, all will be well in less than a week."

"Do you think it wise, my lord? Someone might have recognized you."

He studied the man he had trusted for the last five years to hold some of his secrets. Atterly was a bastard, in deed and name. He did not have a care who was hurt, as long as he got paid. They shared that common trait. Lord knew he had creditors foaming at the mouth to get a piece of him. Atterly though, never seemed to want for money. He didn't seem to care about material things. He just cared about amassing a fortune.

"No. If anyone saw me, they would be loath to admit they had been in such a place. And truly, who would believe one of those people over me? I am not known for coming to White Chapel. Don't worry."

He settled back against his seat. His mind turned to the plans. Daniel would have no idea what awaited him. It would be sweet to watch the son of his enemy die.

Chapter Four

"Mum, do you think it be warm enough to go outside soon?"

Anna smiled down at the cherub sitting next to her as she sat down to read a story. Brody was one of their newest children found living on the streets just three months ago. She was happy to see his cheeks had filled out. He had been a skeleton when he had arrived, and afraid of his own shadow.

"You call her, my lady," Jason whispered with enough condemnation to make Brody blush.

"Either is fine with me. And as for the weather, I am not quite sure, but it cannot be soon enough. I look forward to walks in the park."

"We aren't allowed in the park," Brody said.

Once again, she was struck by how little fun these children had before arriving at St Mark's. Everything she had experienced in her childhood that she had taken for granted was mostly unknown to these boys. The adventures in the country were some of her favorite memories. To think that many of them had never walked through a field in spring, or felt the air rush toward their face as they flew down a snowy hill.

"That is just silly. Of course you can go to the park."

She had done just that the last few years. She could not understand the need to hide these children away, then thrust them out into the world. Besides, who could resist a warm spring day at the park?

"One of my favorite things to do when I was your age was go to the park. I was too accustomed to running wild through the village to sit in a London townhouse. I even would get in trouble for going out without my shoes on."

Their eyes widened. "Gor, my lady, I cannot see you doing that."

She laughed. "I did things like that a lot, in fact I still do at times."

"Do you think we can go to the park?"

She looked down at the hope in Brody's bright green eyes. "I will have to see what I can arrange. We do every year." She opened the book. "Why don't we find out just what Mr. Crusoe is up to today, shall we?"

By the time luncheon rolled around, Anna had read two chapters, dealt with a couple of young ladies found out in the cold the night before and sent a summons around to Dr. Timms to come check them for frostbite.

"I hear the children are abuzz about going to the park," Mrs. Markham said.

Anna smiled. "I could not help it. I know we have weeks left before we can go."

"My lady, I rarely step in to say anything..."

"But?"

"Well, you should not get their hopes up."

"Who said their hopes will be dashed. If we have to walk them there, we will get to the park. But I doubt it will come to that. I can usually squeeze some money here and there, and if not, I will use my own money. There needs to be more frivolous activities. And you know that I seem to find a way every year."

The older woman frowned, trying to act the matron, but she

broke down and smiled. "I hope you can do it, my lady."

"I intend to." Even she heard the determination in her voice. These children deserved that much.

She walked to the door to her office. "I think I will get some paperwork done before heading home for the day."

"Oh, my lady, there is a gentleman in your office."

She paused. "One of the benefactors?"

"No. This one I have not seen before, but I recognized the name."

She handed Anna the card.

Lord Daniel Bridgerton.

Her pulse jumped, as did her heart. Oh, bother, what was he doing here today? She was still tired from the night before, exhausted from the constant chatter and nonsense of the ton activities. She'd barely slept a wink before rising to attend to her normal activities at the orphanage. The idea that she had to now pull herself together to face Daniel was almost too much to bear.

Mrs. Markham cleared her throat, bringing Anna back from her musings.

She offered the matron her best smile. "He is a good friend of the family. I guess I will have to see what he wants."

She straightened her shoulders, drew in a deep breath, and turned the knob.

Standing by the window, with the weak winter sun blazing around him, was Daniel. She said nothing for a moment and took time to study him. He was the epitome of the well-dressed gentleman. This was not the man she had met years ago. He'd been really little more than a boy, just ten and eight, full of himself and ready to take on the world. Still, with all his arrogance, he had been kind to her. That was why his behavior when she had arrived in town hurt so badly.

With some effort, she pushed those feelings aside. She wasn't the girl she was then.

"Daniel?"

He turned and his golden gaze traveled down, taking in the serviceable gray bombazine dress she wore. It wasn't at all fashionable, but she didn't volunteer at St Mark's to be fashionable. She needed sturdy clothes to be able to do the work. But for once, she wished she had worn something fun and frivolous.

By the time he brought his attention back to her face, his eyes had darkened. It was the same look that he'd had the night before...and it had the same effect. Her pulse raced and she felt slightly faint. There was something about the study that made her think he knew exactly how she looked without her clothes on. Even just the thought had her blushing. She opened her mouth to say something but he stepped forward, formality in his movements.

"Lady Anna."

She wondered at his formality when she realized Mrs. Markham was standing behind her.

"Could you check on when Dr. Timms will be here?"

Mrs. Markham eyed Daniel as if he were the devil incarnate then looked at Anna. "If you insist."

She closed the door behind her leaving the two of them in uncomfortable silence.

"I would be lying if I said I wasn't surprised to see you here."

For a moment, he said nothing. He just kept staring at her. She could not help the feeling that he was measuring her in some way. She had to fight the need to fidget. She opened her mouth to ask him if something was wrong, but he seemed to shake himself out of his stupor.

"Yes, I apologize for not making an appointment."

She laughed as she waved to one of the two chairs in front of the desk. "Making an appointment is unnecessary for you. Please, have a seat." She walked around her desk, trying to put the massive wood barrier between them. Her pulse had tripled and she felt another rush of heat fill her face. Oh, to not be so fair that her blushes showed.

"You will find that we are not very formal here."

Once they had both settled, he stared at her again. Her whole body heated as he continued studying her. She had to resist the urge to check her appearance. Instead, she clasped her hands on the desk in front of her.

"Was there something you wanted?"

That seemed to pull him out his stupor. "Yes. I was just by your house."

Alarm lit through her. "Everyone is all right?"

"Oh, yes, I apologize for alarming you. I thought it best to take this up with Sebastian first."

She frowned. "What did you need to take up with Sebastian?"

"Your work here."

That caught her off-guard. "My work?"

He hesitated. "I had no idea that you came down here on a regular basis."

"And?" she asked when he said nothing else.

"It is not proper."

For a moment, her brain could not seem to work out what he said. Then, when she did, she laughed.

He frowned. "I am serious."

"Yes. I can tell you are serious, that is why I am laughing."

"One might get the wrong idea about a woman who spends so much time in White Chapel."

His implication hit her square in the chest and her laughter died. *Of all the nerve.* She wanted to pick up a pencil and hit him square in the forehead with it. But she resisted...barely. It was what the old Anna would do. Instead, she counted backward from ten, curled her fingers into the palm of her hand and moderated her speech.

"I think you might want to rethink your comments."

At her tone, he narrowed his eyes. "I don't think it is right."

She could feel her spine straightening, her temper boiling. "I did not ask. Nor do I care what you say."

Surprise passed over his expression.

"And furthermore, I take exception at the idea you felt you needed to discuss this with my brother. Considering both of your behavior for years, I hardly think either of you have the right to even think of saying anything to me."

Frustration dripped off him as he rose and paced to the window. "You do not understand the dangers here."

"Do I not?"

He looked at her but she was not in any mood to hear his thoughts on the subject. She allowed some of her temper to show when she continued. "I have worked here for the last two and a half years. I know exactly what goes on around here. How can I not?"

"A woman of your class should not be exposed to it."

She let out a snort. "How pompous you sound. I would have never thought this of you. I have never known you to be so snobbish."

"I understand your need to work with charities, but I think you take this a step too far."

The anger that had been simmering exploded into fury. But she would not show it to him, not to any man. She would not lose her composure in front of him. She had worked very hard to learn to moderate her actions and her emotions.

"I am not the type of woman who is going to sit home and give money to make myself feel better. My mother did not raise me that way. And for your comments about the area, I know what goes on here. Everyone who has spent time in London knows. What makes me different is that I do not turn a blind eye to it. I know that whores work the streets and that children are often preyed upon. That is nothing new. But I cannot live with myself if I do nothing to help."

He studied her for a moment and she saw something shift in his expression. "What you do here is admirable. But even the most optimistic know that it is but a drop in the bucket. It barely counts."

She stood but did not move from her desk. If she did, there was a good chance she would kick him in the shin. "If I save one child from a fate that will leave them damaged...or worse, then it is worth it. My safety is never in question. Sebastian hired two enormous guards."

He frowned. "Your brother said as much."

"Well, at least he has finally accepted that. Just how did you find out about me working down here?"

He hesitated, then grimaced. "Lady Johanna."

Of course, his paramour. His uncle's widow. The woman he left with the night before, just after he had been dancing with her. Pain bubbled in her chest, but she refused to let him know how much it hurt her. She had allowed a man to have that power over her before, and she refused to have that happen again.

"If that will be all, I need to finish some reports before I can head back home for luncheon and I am hungry."

She strode to the door and opened it, waiting for him to walk through it.

In silence, he gathered his hat and approached her. He paused when he stood next to her. She could feel his body heat, smell the scent she always associated with him. Her body hummed, that was nothing new. It took every ounce of her control to look him in the eye and keep her face as blank as possible. He searched her gaze.

"I did not mean to offend. I thought you might not understand the dangers."

"Believe me, I know too well the perils of growing up in the area, my lord."

He nodded but said nothing as he left. She shut the door behind him and leaned against it. Anger still simmered, but mixed with it was pain. She should not be hurt that Daniel had a paramour, or that it seemed his choice lacked morals. But it did. The idea that they were discussing her and her activities was too absurd to be true. Still, where would he have heard it? And why was she feeling as if she had been wronged in some way? He was not her husband or betrothed. It was not as if she thought he would have ever been interested in marrying her.

She walked to the window and watched as Daniel emerged from the door below and out onto the street. The image she had of him when she was a girl just did not match with the man he was. She had thought him more a knight in shining armor, a man who would rescue her. Of course he wasn't. He was like most men, only interested in the next fun activity, the next available widow. She could not respect a man who led a life like that.

Even knowing everything she did, she could not help the way her body shimmered with heat as she watched him stride to his coach. He paused with his foot on the first step and looked up at the window where she stood. She had to resist pulling herself back to hide that she had been watching him. It would have done no good. He gave her a good frown before ducking inside of his carriage.

She watched his coach as it rumbled down the street. With no other diversions, she turned her attention to the budget reports she needed to prepare for the committee that oversaw the orphanage.

Daniel was still fuming when he stomped up the steps of Joanna's townhouse. He slammed the knocker and crossed his arms over his chest. Sylvester answered the door.

"A bit early in the day for you, my lord," he said, his sarcasm easy to hear. Daniel ignored him as he strode past him and down the hall to the kitchen. He knew that it was where to find everyone in the household at luncheon.

He could not be cordial. He had dragged himself out of bed that morning, his head and body still sore, his mind still whirling with visions of Anna. It had been years since he'd dreamed of her, but last night they had returned with vengeance. He could still hear her sighs, feel her flesh, and just the way it had felt sinking into her sweet honeypot.

Bloody, bloody hell. He could not get that image out of his mind. It had taken every bit of his control not to force her to leave that orphanage, away from the filth of those streets. Knowing he had no right did not help the matter. After the ill-fated trip, his head was pounding and his temper frayed. He barged through the kitchen door and found Joanna sitting at the table with her servants. Her eyes widened.

"Please, do come in, Daniel."

He shot her a look that most people would cower before. She smiled.

"You do not want to try to irritate me today." He bit out each word, trying to hold on to his temper.

"From the looks of things I don't need to try."

He opened his mouth but Macy, Joanna's cook, shoved a plate into his hands. "Eat."

He looked down at the meat pie and frowned. "I am not in the mood."

"Every man is in the mood for food."

"And other things, huh?" Walt, her husband, said, wiggling his eyebrows.

"You two behave," Joanna said with amusement threading her voice. "Lord Bridgerton is having a bad day."

With a grumble, he took the seat opposite her and dug into the meat pie. As usual, it was amazing, the delicate flaky pastry and the savory meat fairly melting in his mouth. He had tried more than once to steal her away from Joanna, but her staff was much too devoted to her.

"Now, do you want to tell me what this is about? Did you have a falling out with Lord Michaels again?"

He grumbled as he took a drink of ale that Cook had put down in front of him.

"No. I have not been by there."

Her eyes narrowed. "You said you would take care of that this morning."

"I will take care of it this afternoon. This was...personal."

He felt, rather than saw, the servants shift away to leave the two of them alone.

"Personal. Hmm, if I were to guess, I would say this has to do with Lady Anna."

His head shot up. Her smile grated on his already frayed nerves. He glared at her.

She laughed. "Ah, so it is Lady Anna. What happened?"

"I went down to that...orphanage to tell her that she should not be there."

A suspicious snort erupted as Joanna covered her mouth. She cleared her throat. "And just what did Lady Anna have to say to that?"

The image of Anna, her face flushed with temper, her gaze direct and burning, came to mind. He had not seen her show that much emotion since before the entire episode with Dewhurst. She had looked amazing. He had known she had passion, but now he was sure of it. It was embarrassing just how it had affected him. Even now, he could feel his blood heat, his cock stiffen. He shifted in his seat.

"She read me the riot act. Then she had the audacity to point out that it wasn't any of my business."

"I have to agree with her."

"I only went to her because Sebastian refused to do anything about it."

Jo's mouth fell open before it snapped shut. "Please tell me you did not go to her brother."

He offered her a bland look, and this time she did not hold back the laughter.

"I am so happy that I could bring joy to your world today."

Disgusted with her, with himself, he picked up his plate and took it to the sink. He knew better than to leave his dirty dishes around in this house. Cook had strict policy and she did not care if he was a peer of the realm, she would smack him in the back of the head for leaving a dirty dish on her table.

"What did you think would happen?"

"That she would listen to me. As she should."

Silence greeted that comment. He turned around and found her staring at him, one eyebrow raised.

"You think you decree it, she should follow? For what reason?"

"I am a..."

He trailed off when she narrowed her eyes at him. "What? A man?"

He opened his mouth, but like with Anna earlier, she rolled right over him. "Is this why you think you have the right to kill Duchovny? Because you are a man? My right as a widow is more important, but you are overruling me because you are a man. It is not right."

"In this case, it is important you stay objective. I am not sure that you can."

"If I were a man and Harold had been my wife, would you object?"

"No, that—"

She stood and marched past him. "I am sick to death with men thinking they know everything and that we are the weaker sex."

With that, she stormed out of the kitchen, slamming the door behind her and leaving him alone.

Women. From his mother, to Anna to Jo...he could not win. They were the bane of his existence. He could not say or do anything right today. He needed to escape to his club to avoid any more contact.

Chapter Five

Later that day, Anna set out to scrub the floors of one of the boys' dormitories. She needed something to work off her temper. All day long, all she had thought about was her confrontation with Daniel. She was sick to death of the men in her life trying to protect her from the world. Granted, Sebastian had given up on her a year or so ago, but Daniel...

Well, it made her madder than when Sebastian did it. Sebastian was her brother and would always see her as a girl. But Daniel, he was a man, one she was not related to by blood. The fact that he saw her as a young girl pushed her temper higher.

"Anna?"

Anna looked up to find her cousin smiling down at her. Cicely, Duchess of Ethingham looked every bit of her station today. The fine wine-colored travelling dress was made of the best fabrics. Her once solemn brown eyes now danced with happiness.

"Cicely." Anna rose from her position on the floor. "I would hug you but..." She held out her hands.

"Oh, goodness. A little soap and water won't hurt." Cicely stepped forward and pulled Anna into her arms. The warmth in her voice and in her embrace was the same as always. It had been the one thing she had salvaged from her mistake years earlier. When she finally let go of her, Anna stepped back. "Is there something you needed?"

Cicely nodded. "Can we talk in your office?"

Anna would not be rude. She might not understand why her cousin never blamed her, but she would never be rude to her.

"Follow me. I need to clean up."

Mrs. Markham stepped into the hall.

"Could you be so kind as to get the bucket from the hall? Have one of the lads carry it down. You do not need to be carrying anything so heavy down those stairs."

"I could say the same for you, my lady."

She wanted to snap at the older woman, but she could not. Anna knew she was only looking out for her safety, even if she did try to treat her too kindly from time to time.

Anna continued on to her office, hoping that Cicely was following her.

"I do apologize for being indisposed when you arrived."

Cicely said nothing as Anna dried her hands and then pulled down her shirt sleeves. She must look like a mess. She knew for a fact her hair was in disarray.

"I did not know that you had such duties around here."

Anna finished her task then looked at her cousin. "Our regular cleaning lady for the day is sick, influenza. So I took over her duty. If not, Mrs. Markham would be down there on her knees. She is getting too old for that. But I will swear I did not say that if you tell her."

Cicely laughed. "She reminds me of a dragon whenever we cross paths."

"She is very protective of the boys."

"And of you."

That caught Anna's attention. "Yes, well. What is it that you needed?"

She motioned to the chair in front of her desk.

"I know that Douglas let the cat out of the bag the other night to several people, I assumed he said something to you about the baby?"

Anna nodded.

"Oh, good. We would like you to be godmother."

Anna felt her eyes widen. "Godmother."

"Of course. Colleen was there for Frederick, and we would like to have you to be the godmother of this precious one. Douglas is telling me it is a boy again, but if you must know, I secretly think he wants a girl. I know from the way he treats Colleen and Sebastian's Millicent, he wants a little girl to spoil. You know how Douglas likes to be surrounded by adoring women." Her eyes danced. "But I will not complain because I would love to have a girl."

Anna's ears buzzed as Cicely continued on, talking of her pregnancy, the plans they had for the rest of the year, the plans for the baptism.

"Cicely, excuse me."

Her cousin broke off in midsentence and stared at her. "Is there something wrong?"

"Why?"

"Why do I think that Douglas would want a girl, or why are we leaving London soon?"

Anna waved both questions away. "No. Why me?"

Cicely's face softened. "Anna, dear, you are my friend. When I thought I did not have a friend in the world, you were there."

The pain of that, knowing that she had betrayed her cousin, was more than she could handle. "Only to help trap you."

The sweet biddable look dissolved from Cicely's face. Her

frown had Anna blinking. "I do not want to hear such foolishness from your mouth, do you hear me?"

Her harsh tone should have been for Anna's actions three years ago, not for questioning her behavior now.

"But—"

Cicely rose to her feet and glowered at her. "No. I do not want to hear any excuses. Do you want me to think that you hate me?"

"Hate you? Why would I hate you?"

Cicely smoothed her hands down the front of her dress. Regret filled her eyes. "Your whole problem started because of my actions. I daresay that you would be married now if it had not been for me."

From her tone, Anna realized that Cicely truly thought she had caused Anna's problems. "It isn't true. Truly, Cicely, I hate to think you have been worried about that."

She rounded the desk and took her cousin's hands. "I have not been anything but happy for you. Those mistakes were mine to make. I was a bit of an empty-headed twit."

"Oh, I do not believe that. You were in love."

She had thought she had been. When his betrayal had come to light, the pain of her stupidity had been almost too much to bear. But now, looking back, she was not sure she truly loved him. "Whatever it is, it is past. I do not spend my time down here as a type of penance as everyone believes. I love my work here. I feel like I have accomplished something good."

Cicely squeezed her hands then tugged her in for a hug. "I just want you to be happy, cousin." When she pulled back from the embrace, she was alarmed to see tears in Cicely's eyes.

"Oh, don't cry."

Cicely shook her head. "No, I get a little emotional during this time. I really hate watering up like this."

She took out a handkerchief and blew heartily into it. The rather loud sound made both of them laugh.

"Douglas really does not know what to do with me when I am like this. The man cannot handle the sight of female tears."

"I will have to remember that next time I ask for a donation."

Cicely laughed. "Do that. And please, come more often. Frederick misses you something horrible when you are not around."

"I shall."

After seeing Cicely to the door, she walked back to her office, her mind on the conversation. She should have seen that her actions would make Cicely think she was mad at her. There was no way she could ever blame her cousin for what happened. When Dewhurst had turned her head with pretty words, it had been her own fault. She wished she could say that she had been in love and lost her head. That was what everyone thought. What she let them believe. But deep in her heart she knew the reason she had even allowed Dewhurst to court her was to spite Daniel.

Those few weeks had been a dream come true. She'd had men pursue her before, but not so...ardently. Being young and hurt by Daniel's rejection, she had wanted nothing but true love. She had tried, tried so hard to be in love with Dewhurst, but there had always been another there. In the back of her mind, she had compared everything Dewhurst did, from the way he walked and talked to his dancing, to Daniel. The worst part of the whole mess was that everyone thought she was in love with the man, trying to mend a broken heart. The truth of the matter was that she had almost lost her cousin because she had been trying to prove something to herself. That she could fall in love with a man other than Daniel.

She had failed. In a twist of fate, the man had not been in love with her either. She'd just been a means to an end. For the sake of pride, she had almost gotten her cousin killed.

She closed her eyes and fought her way back to reality, to the present. Thinking about the past did her no good at all. She had accounts to balance before she left.

Anna paused in bringing her teacup to her mouth when Daniel walked through the door of her mother's day room. It had been three days since the scene at the office, and she had been thankful that he had not returned. It seemed that her reprieve was over.

"Good day, Lady Anna," he said.

For a moment, she did not respond. It was decidedly odd that he not only appeared for tea, but in her mother's day room.

"Sebastian is in his study."

"Ah, yes, well."

For the second time in just a few days, he seemed to be at a loss for words. It was completely out of character for Daniel. His intense stare had every nerve in her body shimmering with heat.

She took a sip of tea before asking, "Is there something you wanted?"

Everything in him seemed to still, his whole body going rigid. He visibly swallowed then cleared his throat. Growing concerned, she rose. "Daniel?"

He took a step back when she started for him, so she stopped. "Uh, I just wanted...to ensure that there were no hard feelings between us."

Of course. He was worried about their friendship. She forced herself to smile. "Daniel, there have always been hard feelings between us."

"Come now, there was a time when we had camaraderie between us. I believe I did help you sneak out of your lessons more than once."

She laughed, remembering her childhood friend and the way he had understood her need to escape. "Yes, I do remember more than once or twice sneaking out of lessons to ride. My mother has never been able to discover who helped me out of the house. She has always blamed Sebastian for it."

The smile that curved his lips did delicious things to her insides. "You mean to say you have never told anyone who helped you. I thought with your..."

She shot him a wry look as she moved back to her seat. "Big mouth? Yes, I used to be a bit of a tattler...especially where Sebastian was considered. He seemed to get away with too much in my opinion."

"When we were at Eton he would regale all of us of your ability to get him into trouble."

"Oh, really." She assumed Sebastian had complained, but to think he whined to his friends made her laugh. "I can see him now, all injured pride being caught trying to tup one of the local girls."

The moment it came out of her mouth, she regretted it. Daniel's eyes narrowed and he stepped closer. "That he did not tell us. And really, Anna, what language."

"I learned it from you or Sebastian, that I am positive about."

"I do not think so. I knew better than to say things like that around impressionable young ladies."

"I wasn't an impressionable young lady. I was a pesky brat who ruined all your plans by tagging along."

He cocked his head to one side. "I want to hear about this local girl."

"It was really all by accident. Nanny Alice was sick and I had the day off, and it was a glorious day." She closed her eyes, remembering the day, the heat of the sun on her face, the feel of grass under her feet. Anna liked London, but she truly enjoyed country life.

"Anna?"

She opened her eyes, puzzled by the strange tone in his voice.

"The story."

"Oh, yes. Well, I saw Sebastian heading toward the stable, and I thought it odd because he told me earlier he didn't have time for a ride. And come to think of it, he smiled when he said it." She shook her head. "I was hurt that he had decided to go off on his own. So I followed him to the pub, which I knew he wasn't supposed to go to. But then he came out with one of the miller's daughters and they snuck off to her father's barn. I followed."

He cleared his throat and she smiled. "I did not have one clue what was going on. What I did was call attention to them. Everyone came running into the barn, thinking I was hurt. Sebastian came running down to save me, straw in his hair and his shirt undone. When word got back to Mother, she was not amused."

"I cannot believe you have not told me of this before."

She smiled at him over her cup. "I can keep secrets. Why does no one think I can?"

He took the seat opposite her and studied her. "It is because you are honest. Your emotions show on your face."

She truly hoped that was not true. Everything in her seemed to be shimmering with some unexplainable heat. It was always like this, but the past few days, it had been growing. Just thinking about him, the way it had felt to have his hands on her... Oh, bother. When would she outgrow this silly fascination with the man? She had thought she had. But the last few nights she had dreamed of him, of having him in her bed...touching her.

Silently, she cursed herself. Would she ever learn? He did not see her as a woman, just Sebastian's pesky little sister. After arriving in town and being treated as if she had the pox, she had vowed to ignore him. It had been difficult because the man was constantly in their house. Whenever their paths did cross, it erupted into an argument. If she had said the sky was blue, Daniel would say it was green. And vice versa. Until the last few years. Then they had seemed to just...avoid each other.

"Oh, so those of us who are honest cannot keep secrets. I think you do not know of which you speak."

His smile faded, his gaze turning cold. "I know more than you would ever want to know about it."

The air around them seemed to still, his serious tone pulling any heat out of the room. She shifted in her chair, uncomfortable with the way he was looking at her.

"But then you say you never told your mother about the times I snuck you out of the house, if you are to be believed." His tone told her that he didn't.

"I assure you that I did not. First you say that I cannot keep a secret, now you are accusing me of lying."

"Hmm." He continued to stare at her as if trying to delve into her mind and discover what she was thinking.

"Do you think if my mother knew you were the one who snuck me out of the house that she would not have said something? There is one thing my mother would not allow and that is not letting someone know just what she thinks."

That made him laugh and the air between them softened. "That I have to agree with. Your mother is as much of a harridan as my own."

Had it been anyone else she would have taken exception to the comment. There was a wealth of warmness in his voice that spoke of his admiration for both women.

"Truly, if I were married with children and my mother was

told of some transgression I had done when I was a child she would make sure I knew of it," Anna said.

"You should, you know."

Again he turned serious. She could not seem to keep up with his changing moods. This was so unlike the man she had known over a decade, she could not understand him.

"I should what?"

"Marry. Have children."

The subject instantly brought a rush of tears to her eyes, but she blinked them away and looked outside. She knew if she looked at him she would let the tears fall. It had been the one thing she regretted about her mistake three years earlier. She had always wanted a horde of children.

"I would rather not talk about it."

"You cannot spend the rest of your life paying for what happened."

She sighed. "I said I did not want to talk about it." She cut him a sharp look. Anger flashed over his face. Lord Bridgerton was not accustomed to being told no.

"As you wish." He rose from his seat and she followed suit. "I must speak to Sebastian. Thank you for the conversation."

She nodded and watched him leave. When he reached the doorway, he turned to study her for a long moment. "You would make a wonderful mother, Anna."

In the next moment, he was gone, not allowing her to respond to him. She sank onto the settee and blinked, trying to keep the tears at bay. She rarely thought of what she was missing by choosing the path she had, but just hearing Daniel make the comment brought it all to the forefront.

The one man she might break her promise for had just told her that she would make a good mother. It was enough to make a woman weep.

Daniel escaped to Sebastian's study, thankful he had avoided any of the other women in his house.

"You seem to be out of sorts."

Daniel tossed his best friend a mean look but said nothing else as he poured himself some tea.

"Did you and Anna have a fight?"

"No." He knew he was terse, and he didn't give a bloody damn. He itched from the inside out. There was something there, something in that sad expression Anna had that told him she still hurt...still longed for that bastard. Anger whipped through him, barely contained. He wanted to destroy something. He felt so inept, so impotent. If the bastard had not killed himself years ago, Daniel would gladly hunt him down and kill him for hurting Anna. For the first time in years, he had almost lost it, almost gone to her and pulled her into his arms.

When she hurt, he did too.

And that alone was enough to drive him insane.

"Please, don't talk so much. You might overwhelm me."

Daniel sighed. "If you must know, I apologized."

"For what?"

"For telling her that she should not be working down in White Chapel."

Sebastian chuckled. "Ah, yes, I was told of your visit."

"Excuse me?"

"I have to thank you for that because you made me look like a good brother. She was none too happy with you."

He set his tea on the table beside him and stared at his friend across the expansive desk. "Indeed?"

"What do you think you were about?"

"I am not sure now. Everyone seems to think I have lost my

mind." And he was beginning to think he had. Why else would he seek the woman out when being in her company was so painful?

"I have to agree."

"You mean to tell me you aren't worried about what she does?"

"Of course I am, but I know better than to try and stop her. If I forbid her, you know the result of that. She would just go around me, and without any protection."

That was true. From the moment he had met Anna she had never been one to sit idly by and allow things to happen around her. She had always jumped into the middle of the activity and enjoyed. He shifted in his seat, avoiding Sebastian's probing gaze. After his encounter with Anna, his emotions were too open, too raw. He could not believe that she had not divulged who helped her those years earlier. He had indulged in befriending Sebastian's younger sister because she seemed to enjoy the things he did too. They both thrived in the country and they had a special affinity for horses. And he had never met a girl quite like her. She loved adventures, but she was still feminine. They had remained friends until he'd attended her coming-out ball. Then it had become impossible.

"Truthfully, I was hard pressed to tell her no three years ago. You remember what she was like. Not only had she lost a man she thought to marry, but she put a cousin she dearly loves in danger because of it. It was a bit too much to bear for her."

"And so you allowed her to go traipsing around an area filled with whores and beggars?"

One eyebrow rose at his tone and he could understand that. He sounded as if he felt he had a right to her.

"You forget just how broken she was. The fact that she showed any interest was enough for me. I could not let her sit here and waste away. What did you expect me to do?"

"I do not see what the bloody hell she thinks she is doing."

"I believe I heard all of this a few days ago. And since you seem to either be hard of hearing or are starting to lose your memory in your old age, I will remind you of what I said. I might disagree with her being in such a dangerous part of town but, believe me, she does very good work there. Why, she practically manages the orphanage, and I am sure that is not something any of us expected of her three years ago."

He could not argue with that. After leaving his argument with Joanna, Daniel had started to dig into the background of the orphanage and had found that Anna was not only their primary benefactor, she did a lot of their fundraising. It was a lot for any person, not to mention a young woman who had no training or background for it.

"Why do you seem so interested in this? Do you not think I can protect my sister?"

"Of course I do. I just feel...protective, as I do with my sisters."

One of Sebastian's eyebrows rose as he studied Daniel. After a few beats of silence, Sebastian said, "Indeed. Well, I assure you that even if she were in trouble without escort, she would have help from the locals in the area. She has gained the respect of many of the inhabitants. Several of them would probably slit your throat if they thought you were a threat to her."

"And you are comfortable that she spends her time with these people?"

Sebastian blew out a sigh filled with exasperation. "Good God, man, let it be. She is protected and won't get into any trouble. She has been there for over two years working without a hint of trouble."

He wanted to argue, but he could see speculation in

Sebastian's gaze. One thing he did not need was her brother wondering just why he was so interested. He would make sure that nothing happened to her even if her brother did not.

Sebastian watched his friend climb into his carriage and sighed. There was something decidedly odd with Daniel's behavior. There had always been something Daniel kept from him, some secret he did not want Sebastian to know. He did not think it were illegal, Daniel was much too honest for that. But there was something there that seemed to occupy much of his time, especially these last few months.

The door opened and shut behind him. He did not need to turn around to see who it was.

"Was that Daniel?" Colleen asked as she slipped her arms around his waist and rested her head against his back.

"Yes. He has taken a bit of interest in the comings and goings of Anna."

"Hmm."

Without breaking contact, he turned around and pulled her close. "What does that mean?"

She widened her eyes innocently. "Whatever do you mean?"

"Do not even try to play me, Colleen."

"I saw them dancing the other night."

When she did not continue, he knew her clever mind was working something out. "And?"

"There seemed to be something between them."

He jerked back and looked down at her. "You're mad. Daniel thinks of her as a little sister."

She said nothing else but gave him one of those irritating looks.

"Colleen?"

She smiled, one that never failed to seduce him. "So, my

lord. You have some empty time on your hands this afternoon?"

Heat and love slipped through him as he leaned his head down to brush his mouth over hers. His worries about his best friend were easily forgotten as he set about loving his wife.

By the time Daniel arrived home later that night, all he wanted to do was climb into his bed. His day had started early and gone downhill fast. His meeting at the docks had gone as well as he expected. Meaning it had been a mess.

The door opened and Higgens stood beside it, an anxious look on his face.

"My lord. We had a problem arise."

Daniel sighed as he stepped over the threshold of his townhouse. "Of course we have. What is it now? Mother complaining because I did not attend tonight's festivities? The way I smell she probably would understand."

"Good God, Daniel, what on earth happened to you?"

He looked down the hall to find his mother gaping at him.

"I decided to take a dip at the docks." He strolled into his study. If he was going to deal with smelling like rotted fish and his mother, he needed brandy. "Really, Mother, you would think after all the years you have spent as a spymaster's wife you would be accustomed to this."

"It is quite different when it is one's husband."

He took a stiff drink and studied his mother. She had not dressed to go out which raised his suspicions. But there was something wrong. She was pale, a frown marring her brow.

"What happened?"

She went over to his desk and pulled a piece of paper out of the drawer. She hesitated before giving it to him.

"Mother."

There were still times, even after all these years, that she tried to shield him from the truth.

She gave up and handed him the letter. He didn't see much at first, but he saw the signature. It was a name that had haunted him since he was a lad of ten and three.

The Viper.

"It is him." His mother's voice shook when she spoke.

He looked at her and he realized the fear was very real. And for good reason. It was the man who'd killed her husband.

"You must leave London."

He cut her a sharp glance. "You know that is impossible."

"Did you read it?"

He nodded as he searched for clues in the writing but knew there would be little there but threats and demands. And a condescending attitude.

"Well?"

"I understand—"

"You have no children, so you cannot understand."

"I cannot leave London at present. You know that as well as I do."

Tears gathered in her eyes and panic surged through him. His mother did not cry. She did not carry on. She held onto her emotions.

"This is not the end of it."

With that, she turned around and stomped out of the room. Regret filled him at his harsh words, but he could not have his mother dictating what he did. He had too much on his plate now. Joanna seemed convinced her husband's killer was to be in London soon, and he had a problem with someone selling secrets to a French agent and now it seemed that the man who'd killed his father had decided to come out of hiding.

And the one thing he wanted to do was to kill Daniel.

Chapter Six

Anna frowned as she stepped down from her carriage the next morning. Mrs. Markham stood on the front of the steps, a worried expression as she looked up and down the street. Anna drew in a calm breath and walked to the steps of the orphanage.

"Is something amiss?"

Mrs. Markham looked down at her and the fear she saw in the matron's eyes sent a slice of panic inching down her spine.

"Oh, my lady. We had some problems last night."

Anna marched up the stairs. "Problems."

"Someone tried to break in."

Worry turned to outright panic. "Break in? To the orphanage? Why would they do that?"

Mrs. Markham stepped aside to allow Anna inside. It was a drafty old home that had been purchased with funds Anna had practically begged off her acquaintances. But there was something homey about it. She had tried to convey an atmosphere of a regular home since most of the children had never had that luxury before entering the orphanage.

She pulled off her hat as she hurried up the steps to the office.

"Yes, my lady, they tried to fiddle with the door."

She stopped on the step and looked down at the matron.

"Fiddle?"

"They were trying to open the lock."

With her frown deepening, she continued on her way. "Do you have any idea what the reason behind it might have been?"

Anna walked into her office. Several staff members, including their bookkeeper, Mr. Francis, were in deep discussion. She did not have to ask what their subject was. It was easy enough to discern from their expressions.

"What is going on?"

Mr. Francis stepped forward. He was a wonderful man, just two years older than she. He was the son of a wealthy merchant who aimed to step into his father's shoes one day and run their spice business. But his father believed in giving back to the community, and so he had volunteered his time to handle their money.

"My lady. I did not hear of this until I showed up this morning."

He cut a cold look at Miss Richardson, one of their teachers. Her spine stiffened. "I did not see the reason for bothering anyone about it this morning. Mrs. Markham and I were sure the watch would not come down here in the middle of the night and Lady Anna had a board meeting to attend to last night."

She sighed. "I will contact my brother to see what can be done. But I am afraid Miss Richardson is correct. The watch will do nothing unless something happens."

"So they wait until someone is hurt, then they do something." The disgust dripped from Mr. Francis's voice. He had led a sheltered life, perhaps more sheltered than her own. While not a stupid man, there were things he was a bit naive about.

She offered him a shrug. "I am sorry, but that is the way of the world. Thankfully, we have the power of my brother. We will definitely make sure there is someone to take care of things. Now I am sure that all of you have duties to attend to."

Everyone filed out of the room except for Mrs. Markham. The matron closed the door behind them.

"We will have to keep an eye on those two."

Anna paused in sitting down. "Who? Miss Richardson and Mr. Francis. They cannot stand each other."

The older woman laughed. "Where there is emotion there is something else beneath it. Both of them have been at each other the last few weeks."

Anna pulled out a piece of paper to write a note to her brother. "I trust that the children have not witnessed any arguments."

"No."

"Well, hopefully it will blow over."

She chuckled. "The only thing that will help that blow over is a good roll in bed."

Heat filled Anna's face. "Really, Mrs. Markham."

Even after all these years she was not accustomed to her matron's frank talk. Anna guessed that was what happened when you hired a former working girl to be the head of your orphanage.

"I am just speaking plain."

"I do not think it is any of our business. So why don't we discuss what is going on. Do you have any idea why someone would try to break in? I can't see a reason around here."

"That is what is puzzling me, my lady. Most of the residents would never allow someone to even knock on the front door. It had to be someone new, or someone not from the area."

"Hmm. Well, I will send a note to my brother. I am sure we can get someone to watch the area at night to make sure. He can also bend the ear of a few friends and see if we can get more watch patrols."

"Not likely, especially at night."

She smiled at the woman. "It is worth a try."

Mrs. Markham chuckled. "You are always so optimistic. Do you never see the bad in the situation?"

Anna shook her head. "I see the bad. I just think that there is some good in all people."

"I hope you keep that idea, my lady."

Several hours later, Anna hid behind a smile as she finished a country dance. She knew this would happen. Her mother would make her attend more soirees after she attended Cicely's ball. There was not much she could do about it. Complaining would not work, and whining was beneath her. It was little to ask of her. Her family had been very patient and understanding after what she had done. And she thought it might be a good place to raise funds.

Unfortunately, she had been besieged by young men since she had stepped into the ballroom. Young men who did not have control over their fortunes, and most of them could care less about the orphanage. Most other men did not care either, but they were married and their wives did.

"It is good to see you out more, Lady Anna."

She cut a sharp glance at the young man returning her to her mother.

"I go out, Lord Greenwood."

He reddened and swallowed and she instantly felt guilty. He was a nice enough man with a shock of curly red hair, dark green eyes and the sweetest disposition. Unfortunately, even though he was several years older than Anna, she always felt as if she was the older of the two of them.

"I do apologize. I did not mean that you did not do anything. I know that you do a lot of work with your orphanage."

That made her stop in her tracks. "You do?"

He smiled. "My father told me all about it. Apparently, your mother does talk about it."

His father? She had no idea her mother was acquainted well enough to be discussing her daughter with the man. She looked for her mother in the crowd and found her looking up at the Earl of Greenwood with a smile that stunned Anna. She could not remember ever seeing her mother looking like that, not since their father died.

"Lady Anna."

She turned to find a young footman standing beside her. "Yes."

"This came for you a moment ago."

She took the envelope and recognized the penmanship immediately. She tore it open and read the note from Mrs. Markham. Several of the boys were sick. Panic welled up inside of her.

She turned to Lord Greenwood as she ordered herself to calm down. "I do apologize but something has come up. Could you tell my mother that I had to go home?"

There was no reason why she should tell her mother that she had to leave for the orphanage. It would only take a moment to stop by and double check on the boys. Mrs. Markham could take care of it herself, but the truth was the doctors tended to come faster if they knew the summons was from her and if she were in attendance.

"If you are—"

"Nothing all that important, but I need to make sure this staff member is taken care of."

She smiled at him and he seemed to lose his concentration as he stared at her.

"Lord Greenwood?"

He shook himself out his stupor. "Of course, Lady Anna."

She thanked him again, then made her way out of the ball room. If one good thing came out of the illness hitting the children, it had helped her escape early.

Daniel crept down the street ever aware of the danger around them. Yes, meeting a former French spy was dangerous, but Daniel knew the bigger danger was those who inhabited the streets here. They were the lowest form of scum on the earth, and many of them could care less whether they lived or died.

"Do you think there is a chance the froggie will run?" Jack asked.

"I have no doubt he will be here. He owed everyone in town." And he had said he knew of the Viper. That had been enough to pull Daniel away from anything, especially the ball.

When they stepped onto the street, he realized that they were just a block or two over from Anna's orphanage. He would have to come up with something that would keep her out of here. He was not a man who thought women should be sheltered, but running around the East End was just not the thing. Even during the day. He knew he didn't have a right to tell her what to do, but he truly didn't want her hurt. If she continued in this fashion, something would happen.

He pushed those thoughts away. Having a woman, especially this woman, on his mind was not a good thing considering their mission. He had to keep his mind on what was happening around them. As they made their way to the pub, Daniel sensed a stir in the air. It gave him a sense of foreboding before the man stepped out of the shadows.

"I hear there are wolves running loose in London."

Jack jumped, his hulking figure moving toward the man. Daniel stopped him. "No." Then he turned to the man. "You should not pay attention to the gossip of the ton, my lord."

The man stepped into the light and the nerves that had bunched up seemed to relax. Both Jack and he walked toward the man. They were not alone, Daniel was not stupid. He had brought backup, some of his own, some of Jo's.

"I understand you have news of the Viper?"

The man licked his lips. As Daniel moved closer, he realized the man was not that old. A shame for someone so young to be entangled in such a mess. He would not recognize Daniel in his costume, but Daniel knew him. A baron that had come into his fortune early on and squandered it. There was a reason he could sell the secrets to the French. The man's brother worked in the home office.

"Yes. There have been a few people talking."

"And?"

"They say he is back in business. And he has put it out that you are his quarry."

Which made no sense whatsoever. If the man needed the money to spy again, that he understood. But what he did not understand was the man calling him out. Or the way he was making it known he was after Daniel. It was dangerous to him.

"Do you know who this man is?"

He shook his head. "No, but I know he is from the Dover area."

"How?"

But the man was no longer paying attention to him. He looked over Daniel's shoulder out onto the street. "Lord, have mercy." He uttered the whispered plea the moment before a knife flew past Daniel's face and into the man's neck.

Jack was already shouting for their reserves as Daniel turned to face their attacker. Another knife was thrown, catching Daniel in the shoulder. He barely noticed the sting of it as he made his way to the figure standing at the entrance to the alley. It was too dark to see the man, but if he could get closer he might be able to get at least an impression.

When the man realized the number of people flooding the area, he backed away across the street and began running. Daniel tried to chase after him but a carriage pulled in front of Daniel and stopped. His vision blurred and his head began to spin. He blinked twice and tried to focus on the carriage. He recognized the crest as Sebastian's the moment before he sank down on the street.

"Daniel?"

He could not open his eyes, his head fuzzy. The scent of rose water surrounded him as he felt a hand brush against his face.

"Daniel! Jeffries, it is Lord Bridgerton. We must get him inside. Good Lord, he has a knife in his shoulder."

"Ma'am? I think I can take care of him," Jack said.

"And just who are you?" Her voice was filled with indignation.

"I'm his friend."

"Not much of one if you let this happen to him."

Daniel thought he heard snickering.

"Well, all of you need to help me get him up into the carriage."

"But…"

He wanted to tell the men not to let her take him, that it was a risk to her, but his brain did not seem to be able to tell his mouth to function. He opened his mouth but nothing came out. A wave of nausea hit him just as his world faded to black.

Chapter Seven

Daniel returned to consciousness as he was being jostled from the carriage.

"Oh, do be careful. He is an injured man."

"That one does like to tell a man what to do," Jack mumbled under his breath.

"I heard that."

Jack said nothing else but grunted as he stepped down from the coach. The knocker sounded and the door opened.

"We have your lord. He's been stabbed," Anna said.

"My lady?"

"What is it, Higgens?" His mother. Bloody hell, this was getting worse by the minute.

"Ah, it seems that Lord Bridgerton is indisposed." From the sound of Anna's voice she was not pleased his mother was home. He could not blame her.

"Indisposed? Oh, Anna. What in heaven are you doing here?"

"I had to attend to something at the orphanage, and on my way home I came upon Daniel who almost was run over by my carriage."

"And why is Jack carrying him?" his mother asked.

"Well, he passed out and he is too heavy for me to carry. I assumed they were friends."

"Passed out, as in drinking?"

Anna said nothing for a moment, apparently sensing the desperation in his mother's voice. "No. He was stabbed. Jack, if that is the brute carrying him, pulled it out and the bleeding has stopped."

She paused as Jack carried him up the stairs to the front door. With each step, the ache in his shoulder burned, a spark of pain shooting through his body. It took all his energy to keep himself from losing the contents of his stomach right there.

"Stabbed?" His mother's voice had risen, desperation threading her tone. "Bloody hell. Get him inside."

"Lady Adelaide, you need to step aside for us to do that." Anna said the words firmly, but he could hear the compassion beneath it.

"Of course. Higgens, call Doctor Timms."

"Oh, and we will need some good cloths and warm water."

He would not have Anna in his sick room. He would not lose his dignity. It was bad enough how he had embarrassed himself in front of her already. He lifted his head to tell her just that but his vision faded again and he felt himself slip under.

"Thank goodness he passed out again," Anna said.

Lady Adelaide sighed as Jack removed Daniel's shirt. "I am just glad you were there when this happened. Who knows what would have happened."

"We would have taken care of him just fine," Jack said.

She glanced at the man who was a strange companion for Daniel to be sure. He wore simple clothes, his demeanor was as if he worked for the Bridgertons, but she did not recognize him. He was small in stature and had a face that was quite unpleasant to look upon. His gaze moved from side to side as if he were waiting for the next attack.

When he pulled the fabric free of Daniel's body, she gasped. Bruises marred his flesh, bright purple and yellow over his torso. They were at least a few days old.

"What in the world happened to him?"

"Oh, you know boys." Lady Adelaide sounded as if she were trying to avoid the conversation.

"Yes, but he is a bit past the point of being a boy, is he not?" Anger surged at the complacency in the room. It was as if his mother did not care. What in heaven's name was going on? She picked up the cloth and dipped it in the warm water.

"It is decidedly odd because I have never known Daniel to be into that part of town."

"I am sure that he had a reason to be there." Lady Adelaide sounded even more distant than before.

She wanted to argue with her, but the older woman's position, and the fact she was a friend of her mother's kept Anna from doing that. She pressed a cloth gently around the wound to clean it.

"It does not look all that bad. In fact, it isn't that bad at all. A good stitching is all it needs."

"I am glad to hear your analysis, young woman, but I am sure that Lady Adelaide would like to hear from a doctor."

She glanced up at the older gentleman who came into the room. She recognized him immediately. "Dr. Timms. I am sure you are sick of seeing me."

"Lady Anna?"

"Yes. I was checking on the children tonight. We had another one come down with fever, but he is doing just fine. Nothing too high."

He smiled as he came toward her. He was her favorite physician to use and although she knew he only did it because of her position, she truthfully didn't care. He showed a respect for the boys that most doctors did not.

"Ah, well I am here. I will be happy to take over."

She frowned at him, not wanting to leave Daniel. She glanced back down at him, worried about the pallor of his skin. Anna looked up and opened her mouth but Lady Adelaide stopped her.

"Oh my goodness. Look at your dress."

Anna looked down and saw the smudges of dirt and blood on her ball gown.

"Oh, I really hate to see that. Your mother will be wondering what happened." She moved around the bed. "Whatever will you tell her?"

"What do you mean?"

"I would hate for anyone to find out about Daniel. Do you think you could…"

She glanced at the man in question and without hesitation said, "Do not worry, Lady Adelaide. I will tell my mother it is from the orphanage."

She glanced at Daniel one more time and then allowed his mother to hurry her out of the room.

Two days later, Anna listened to her mother complain about her disappearance—again. Anna barely heard her. Since she had left Daniel's townhouse, her mind had been on him…and those injuries. She desperately wanted to send a note to him but knew that would raise suspicions. She thought it horribly rude that Lady Adelaide at least did not contact her. What on earth had Daniel been doing down there? And just what was with all the men he was with? They were not his friends. Some of them looked much older and definitely much more experienced than he. *Stabbed.* She still worried that the wound was much worse than she had thought it to be. What if he lost too much blood? Or what if the hit to his head was worse than she had thought?

"Are you listening to me?"

She glanced at her mother sitting across the room from her. "I understand you were upset. Did I not go to another musicale last night? Since it featured the Tate twins, I deserve something for that."

Her mother offered her a little smile. The Tate twins were notoriously tone deaf. "True. But I want you to understand that your absence was noticed."

Anna rolled her eyes. "And I am sure they all know I left because of the orphanage."

"Yes. Just the thing you need to be known for, traipsing around the slums in the middle of the night."

Anna barely held onto her rapidly fraying temper. Did no one think she had a brain? "I was never in any danger."

"True, I understand that. But men do not want a woman who thinks nothing of running off to take care of children that are not his."

Anna raised her chin. "Then I do not want a man like that. Why would I? I do not want to be a kept woman with nothing better to do than raise her children then bother them about marrying."

Hurt filled her mother's expression. "I am just trying to help."

Regret stirred in Anna's chest. She should have kept her temper under control. She did not want to hurt her mother, because she knew she wanted what she thought best for Anna. But she could not be that girl anymore. She rose and then seated herself next to her mother. She slipped her hands over Victoria's.

"I know, Mother. I know you mean no harm. But I am not sure I can be what any man wants. What I need is to live with my past and create a future I am happy with."

Her mother searched Anna's expression. "Why do you think

that cannot include a husband and children?"

"I am not sure a man would want a wife who feels the need to be involved in my work like I am. It may seem silly to you, but I feel as if I am doing something important at the orphanage. I need to be there."

Her mother studied her and then turned her hands over, taking Anna's between hers. "I need to see you settled."

Anna paused, unable to discern her mother's tone. She had been preoccupied lately. In fact, there were times Lady Victoria had disappeared for hours at a time. But this was different. There was something there she had not heard before, something she could not truly understand. It was as if there was a desperate need beneath those words. What did her mother have to be desperate about?

She opened her mouth, but Starnes interrupted her.

"Lord Bridgerton is here to see you, my lady."

For a moment, her heart stopped. He was fine. In the next, her whole body heated with the thought of seeing him.

"My lady?"

She shook herself out of her stupor. "I will be done in a moment."

Everything in her body seemed to shimmer in anticipation. What was she thinking? Was this because she was worried about him?

She checked herself in the mirror. With a deep breath, she straightened and made her way downstairs. All the way she continued to remind herself to stay calm. This was just Daniel coming by to let her know he was all right.

She reached the bottom of the stairs and noticed one of the footmen.

"Lord Bridgerton is in the front parlor, my lady."

She wanted to run down the length of the hall just to get

there faster, to witness with her own eyes that he was okay. But instead, she forced herself to put one foot in front of the other slowly. When she reached the doorway, she paused and watched him. His back was to her as he looked out the window. Bright sunlight shimmered around him, highlighting the flecks of gold within his hair.

He was fine.

She must have made some kind of noise because he turned around. The moment his gaze rested upon her, she found herself mesmerized. There was something in the way he looked at her that made every thought in her brain dissolve. It had been this way since that waltz the week before. It made her aware of everything in her body—her heartbeat, the prickles that moved over her skin and the overwhelming need to be touched.

"Lady Anna."

She shook herself and ordered her feet to move in the room.

"It is good to see that you are all right."

He grimaced when he moved and instantly, she rushed forward. He put his right arm up to ward her off. "I am fine. I just moved it the wrong way."

Silence filled the air around them. When he said nothing she finally asked, "Whatever happened to you down there?"

For a moment, Daniel could not get his brain to function. He could truly blame it on the medication he had been on, but he knew it had to do with the woman in front of him. Daniel tried to remember the lie his mother had helped him concoct in the wee hours of the morning. There would be no way hiding his injury from most people. But worse, Anna had seen him injured and there was no way avoiding her.

"Jack is the nephew of Higgens."

"Did Jack stab you?"

He smiled. "No. He owed some money and I was trying to help him with the money lender."

Her eyes narrowed. "But you were dressed oddly."

"Well, I could not go down there in my own clothes."

"Why ever not? I would think that would help you more."

Daniel wanted nothing more than to crawl back into bed. His head was still fuzzy from the laudanum. Dealing with Anna in such a state was not a good idea. Even now, with his body aching and his head throbbing, he could feel arousal snake through his blood. She was wearing a simple white day dress with embroidered cornflowers along the neckline. There was nothing truly seductive about it, but that did not seem to matter. It just made him want to peel it away from her body and see what lay beneath.

"Daniel?"

He shook his head. "What?"

"I said, I thought that being dressed in your own clothes would have gained you more respect."

The woman was too clever. He was trying to imagine just what she would look like wearing nothing but the sunlight, and she was questioning him as if she were the head of the War Department, Lord Michaels.

"I did not want to draw attention to us."

She didn't look like she believed him but thankfully she let it go.

"Are you sure you are all right?" The worry in her voice, along with the concern in her eyes did not comfort him. He did not want to be coddled, to be seen as weak.

He nodded. "Just a little scuffle and Doctor Timms said it was not serious."

"Jack works for your family?"

"No, he works for..."

It was then that he realized his mistake. Everyone in the ton thought he was having an affair with Lady Joanna, but for some reason he did not want Anna to think that. But it was too late.

"Yes?"

"Ah, he works for Lady Joanna."

Anna's face paled, her expression going blank. Something in the area of his heart pricked.

"It is not what you think."

"I really have no idea what you are talking about." Ice dripped from her words.

He hated this, hated lying to her, and in this one thing, he would be honest. "Joanna and I are not..."

She had moved away, in body and mind. He walked to her and touched her arm. She shivered and he was not sure if it was the heat or fear.

"Anna?"

She would not look at him and he needed it, needed the connection to her. He touched his forefinger to her chin and moved it up so that she had to look at him. He could not read what she was thinking.

"I promise there is nothing between Lady Joanna and myself. We are friends, nothing more. She is still mourning my uncle's death. Even if she were not, she does not interest me in the least."

He held her gaze for a moment and then allowed for her to pull away. She walked to the window he had been standing in front of a moment earlier.

"She seems your type of woman, Daniel."

"What does that mean?"

She shrugged which angered him. He could not understand

himself, but for some reason, he could take anger from her more than complacency.

"Anna."

She turned to face him and again he could not read her expression. It was something that frustrated him. She had been an open book at one time. But ever since that damned Dewhurst hurt her she had become a mystery. He could never tell what she was thinking.

"What do you mean she is my type?"

"It is not as if I do not hear of your antics around the ton. It was very hard not to hear of it when Sebastian is your best companion. People tend to enjoy throwing your brother's bad behavior in your face to see how you will react."

"Back to the type of woman you think I like."

Her face flushed with color. "Never mind."

"Anna."

"Well, all right. You like dark-haired women with lots of...curves."

He looked at her for a moment. "How do you know that?"

"Oh for goodness sakes, Daniel, everyone knows what paramours you keep, and if I didn't I am sure it would not be hard to figure it out from what plays you attend."

He frowned. Was he that transparent?

"It does not matter in the least. It is your private life. All that matters is that you are not seriously hurt."

He offered her a smile. "Fit as ever."

She did not return the smile. If anything, her expression grew more pensive. "The bruises you had on your chest did not look like they were new. What on earth are you about?"

Damn, his mother had not told him she had been in the room when they removed his shirt. Of course, his mother was not acting in her right mind since that note had arrived from the Viper. She had insisted that he leave again, and when he refused, she'd stopped talking to him.

"That was from a gentleman's boxing match."

She searched his eyes then her shoulders slumped. "If you do not want to tell me, at least do not lie to me." He opened his mouth and she shook her head. "No, you will only lie again."

The sadness he heard in her voice bothered him. Just as he had said days earlier, they had been friendly at one time. Her advancement into womanhood had ruined that. Not because it would not be accepted, but because he could not accept it. From the moment she had arrived he could not keep his mind from wandering into an area where it should not go. It was at that moment he realized just how close he was standing to her. Her body heat warmed his skin and he could smell the rose water she dabbed on her flesh. Oh, that was not a good place to go. But his body did not seem to listen to his mind. Everything in him tensed, hardened. He closed his eyes and the one image that came to mind was Anna, beneath him, naked to his touch.

"Daniel? Are you all right?"

Her voice enticed him. She had always been chatty, but she had one of those deep voices that sunk beneath a man's skin and sent his senses reeling. It was something that he had dreamed of hearing in his bedroom, thick with sleepy passion.

"Daniel!"

The sharpness of her voice had him jolting back into reality.

"Are you sure you are fine?"

He cleared his throat but not the image of her in his bed. His body responded immediately and it took all of his control not to reach for her.

He cleared his throat. "Yes. And I must be going. Mother is not that happy with me at the moment."

She nodded and he turned to go.

"Daniel, are you sure you are going to be all right?"

He looked back over his shoulder at her. "I am."

She said nothing more but let him go. As he jogged down the steps and then stepped up into his coach, he was surprised to find Jack sitting across from him.

"I have a feeling you are going to have a problem with the lady."

"What do you mean by that?" he asked, even knowing the answer.

"According to Jeffries, she might have seen the man who attacked you."

"Who the bloody hell is Jeffries?"

"Her driver last night. He said she asked him if he recognized the man, and when he said he didn't see him, she described what he was wearing."

The implications of her seeing the man playing Viper sent a shiver of panic flushing through his blood. Ice chilled his gut. If Viper saw Anna, if he had recognized the coach, she could be in danger.

"Bloody hell."

Chapter Eight

The moment Anna spotted Daniel approaching her group, she frowned. The musicale she was attending was not thought to be a big attraction to unattached rakes. The men here were either married, like her brother, or too young to tell their mothers no. He barely gave attention to the people who tried to stop him on the way to her. Even as irritated as she was, she could not help the thrill that danced through her blood. What woman would not be? He cut a fine figure in his evening clothes. Daniel was a lean man, all muscle and strength. The crowd unconsciously moved out of his way.

Besides his build, he was a beautiful man. It belied his rather cynical view on the world, but it never failed to gain attention from women—young and old. His gaze never left hers as he methodically moved in her direction. Her pulse hammered in her throat. The way he looked at her, it was as if he owned her.

"Lady Anna?"

She had to bring herself back from her musing to pay attention to Lord Greenwood.

"I do apologize. You were saying?"

He continued talking of his hounds as Daniel muscled his way into her group. She focused on Greenwood. Or tried to. But with Daniel so near, she found herself thinking of other things. Like how he looked without his shirt.

Stop it.

She could not go down that path. But even as she told herself not to, Daniel inched closer. She assumed no one else would have noticed it, but she did.

Finally, Lord Greenwood stopped talking and looked at her expectantly.

"I am sorry, what did you ask?"

"I said that your mother is right excited about the house party my father is throwing."

"Hmm," was all she said before she took a sip of warm lemonade. It was the second time he had mentioned the house party and her mother had yet to say word to her. There was a good chance she planned on kidnapping Anna to make her attend.

The first swipe of a bow across strings was the first indication that the musicale was to start. It was her one chance to escape the crowd for a moment.

"If you gentlemen will excuse me, I need a moment."

All of them nodded but Daniel. She hurried to the retiring room, hoping to escape all of them and possibly much of the performance. She liked music, but sopranos were not her thing. Once she had wasted as much time as she could, she was the last of the women in the area. She stepped out into the hall to find Daniel leaning up against the wall.

"What are you doing here?"

He smiled. "I thought I could escort you back to your seat."

That was a lie because she had no seat and he knew it. Daniel knew she hated sopranos and she did everything in her ability to stay far away from the performance.

"Indeed."

She did not move, but crossed her arms over her chest and tapped her foot. He tried to stare her down but it did not work.

She stayed silent, waiting.

He grimaced. "Dash it, if you must know, my mother made me attend, saying that I owed her an appearance because of the fright I gave her."

That did sound like Lady Adelaide. She was not above using blackmail to get her son to do her bidding.

"What I would like to know is why you are here?"

She widened her eyes. "All young ladies love musicales."

Daniel chuckled, the sound of it sending a shiver down her spine. "Most young ladies, but you hate sopranos."

She made a face. Few people knew her hatred of sopranos...but she only knew the real reason. That she would not tell anyone for all the gold in England. "Truth? My mother made me attend also. It was the only thing I could do to divert her attention from the fact that I ran from the ball last night."

"What were you doing down there?"

He did not have a right to know, but she truly did not care if he did. "A couple of the boys have been ill. Mrs. Markham is a worrier and I had to attend to them. When I show up we are more likely to get a physician there."

"Nothing serious, I hope."

She shook her head. "Just a bit of sniffles, a little fever. They will be right as rain in a few days."

They lapsed into silence as the sounds of the soprano filled the air around them. She could not seem to think of one thing to say, not with him looking at her like that.

"I must get back or Mother will not be happy," Anna said.

He nodded but did not look away. His solemn expression held her captive.

"What? What is it?"

"It has been a long time since you have dressed like that."

She looked down at the ball gown and frowned. "You have

seen me dressed like this before. Why, I was wearing my ball gown the night..."

"Ah, I believe my mother mentioned I ruined it."

"You did not. It was already dirty from attending the boys at the orphanage."

He nodded. But said nothing. Again. She had to resist the urge to fidget, to do something to break his concentration. At the same time, she could feel the excitement rolling through her.

"What?"

He cocked his head to one side. "Am I making you nervous?"

Yes, he was, drat the man. Her pulse fluttered. What was he about? She could not understand his tone. It was one he had never used with her, one that had her body heating. In fact, she had heard him use it for other women...not her. She was never the subject of his hot stares, or his seductive tone.

"Daniel, stop it. I will not be toyed with."

He widened his eyes. "Is that what I am doing with you?"

Anger and embarrassment surged through her, unsettling her stomach. "I...never mind. I must get back. Alone."

She said nothing more as she turned away and walked away, very aware that he watched her every step down the hall.

Daniel waited a few moments before returning. It would not do for people to see him follow her out. Although, that had been what he wanted to do. From the moment he had walked into the musicale and had seen that horde of men surrounding her, he had wanted to do nothing more than to toss her over his shoulder and take her away.

He'd spotted her the moment he'd stepped back into the ballroom. Lord, she was a vision tonight. Blue had always been a good color for Anna. With her flawless ivory skin, the blond hair and blue sparkling eyes, she was a vision in the silk she wore tonight. It hugged every curve, allowing him to appreciate the way she had grown. Anna had always possessed a slight figure, but now there were curves a plenty. Not to mention breasts that were far too exposed for his liking—again. Lord Greenwood was practically drooling on them as he blathered on about his damned dogs. What was her mother thinking letting her out of the house dressed that way?

It hit him in that one moment. Her mother may have enticed Anna to go out to get donations, but she was trying to get the girl married off. Of course she was. Didn't his mother say as much?

It angered him on her behalf. Anna had said she did not want marriage. Did her mother pay no attention to her whatsoever? Of course she did not. Victoria was as much of a meddler as his mother.

"Surprised to see you here," Sebastian said from beside him.

He glanced at his friend. "I wish I could say the same for you. The fact that you do Colleen's bidding is embarrassing."

Sebastian smiled. "The benefits are worth it." Then his smile faded. "I need a moment of your time."

Daniel nodded and followed him out onto the terrace.

"Lord, I hate sopranos."

"It must run in the family," Daniel murmured.

"Ah, yes, Anna hates them too. But then Mother enticed her with the hopes of getting donations from people. From what I gather she has not been able to do any fundraising because of her harem of men who follow her around."

"Yes, of course, that is to be expected with the dress she is wearing."

Something passed over Sebastian's face, but Daniel could

not discern the look he gave him.

"Yes, well, I am here to talk to you about her."

Every fiber of his being tensed. Had Sebastian guessed his regard for his sister? "What is it?"

"There seems to be a problem down at the orphanage."

"Yes, she told me. A couple of the boys were sick."

"No. A few nights ago, someone tried to break into the place."

"Break in? To that orphanage? What would be the reason?"

"I have no idea. I have put a man on it, doing a little digging, but I cannot seem to come up with one motive for a person to want to break into the place. Never mind the fact that the residents are in an uproar about it. They do not take kindly to someone even attempting to hurt something that is linked to my sister."

Sebastian said it with a heavy dose of pride. Daniel understood. There were not that many ladies of her rank who helped with charities, let alone ran the whole place.

"What do you want from me?"

Sebastian studied him for a moment and then said, "I know you have contacts."

His stomach roiled. He had done everything he could to keep things from Sebastian. Not because he did not trust him, but because he needed to protect him. If his enemies thought Sebastian knew anything, they would not stop in trying to obtain information. They would hurt him, his family...anything to gather the information. He opened his mouth to deny it, but Sebastian held up his hand.

"Do not even lie to me. I do not want to know about them. I would never breach your privacy on that matter, but I am asking for you to ask a few of your...associates about it."

He nodded.

"I would be grateful. I am right proud of her work there. She has done a lot and I would hate to forbid her to go because it has grown too dangerous. I am not sure I would succeed anyway."

"I have to agree with you there. Your sister has never been one to listen to the dictates of society."

Sebastian laughed. "Oh, when has anyone in my family done what society dictates?"

Daniel laughed. "I cannot think of the last time you did. Other than marrying your countess."

A fond smile curved his friend's lips and Daniel felt a twinge of envy. The accident that had led to their marriage had been just what Sebastian had needed. And he would be lying if he said he was not jealous of their bliss.

"I will contact a few people, see if they have heard anything. I assumed they would have told me if they had already."

Sebastian frowned. "Why would they?"

Because he had ordered surveillance on the orphanage last week when he had heard she was involved with it, but he could not tell his friend that. It spoke of too much interest.

"They would let me know because of our association."

Sebastian nodded. "Understandable."

The soprano belted out the last few bars of her song. "Good God, that is horrible."

Sebastian laughed. "Yes. Fairly shrivels the goods. I best be getting back."

Daniel nodded as Sebastian drew past him. He stopped and said back over his shoulder, "Take care of yourself, Daniel."

Had Anna told him of his injury? No she would not have told him, thinking to save him from embarrassment. "I always do."

Sebastian nodded and slipped back into the ballroom.

Daniel took a few moments to gather himself and then turned to follow his friend when his mother stepped out.

"You are not behaving, Daniel. You did not even listen to any of the singing."

"Sebastian wanted to talk to me about the orphanage. There seemed to be someone trying to break in the other night."

Immediately, his mother's smile faded. "Nothing serious I hope?"

"They did not get in, but I will have Jack ask around."

She nodded.

"Was there something you wanted?" he asked.

"Yes. I wanted to go to the Fillmores' Ball with Lady Victoria."

"You do not need my permission to go to a ball."

She made a face. "Daniel, behave. I need you to attend to Lady Anna."

"What?"

"Well, Victoria is a little suspicious after last night and is trying to drag the poor girl to the ball. Anna wants to go home."

"Why does she not go with Sebastian and Colleen?"

"They left. Colleen is ill."

"Nothing serious?"

His mother smiled. "I dare say she is increasing again."

"Good Lord, they already have three children."

She chuckled. "I have a feeling you will understand some day. So, will you take her in your carriage?"

The thought had him breaking out in a cold sweat. Alone in a dark carriage with Anna? This would not do. "Do you not think people will question it?"

She laughed. "I doubt it. We are family friends and you are escorting her home. Everyone saw how sick Colleen was."

"How are you getting to the ball?"

"Lord Greenwood is taking us."

"Is he not a little young for you?"

"Not the pup who has been sniffing around Anna's skirts. His father. Really, Daniel, I do not have the time to play around. Will you escort Anna home? She is none too happy with the attention she has been receiving tonight."

Just then he saw her standing off to the side, surrounded by her horde of men. Anger and possessiveness griped him. He did not have a right to it, but he did not like the way they were slavering over her.

"Daniel?"

Without looking away from Anna, he said, "Yes."

"Oh, wonderful." She stepped closer, rose to her toes and brushed her lips over his cheek. "Be careful."

Daniel cursed his mother the moment the door on the carriage shut both he and Anna in alone. Dammit, he should have known better than to let his mother talk him into something like this. They were utterly alone, and he knew with the traffic it would take them close to an hour to get her back to her family townhouse.

"I noticed that you and Sebastian escaped the soprano's performance."

"We could still hear her out on the terrace."

She humphed and crossed her arms beneath her breasts. Even in the dim light he could discern the flesh that rose above her neckline. His fingers itched to glide over her skin, feel it beneath his hands.

He swallowed.

"I daresay it was much worse inside. Why does all of society think sopranos are the type of singer to host?"

"They are known as the epitome of the musical world. They are also known to have volatile tempers and tumultuous affairs. I am certain that some of the young men were there tonight because that soprano is unattached at the moment."

There was a moment of silence. "Oh. I understand now."

Something had shifted in her demeanor, the way her voice sounded. It was like their discussion yesterday at her house.

"What do you understand?"

She did not say anything.

"Anna?"

She sighed. "I noticed that she is your type of woman."

"I told you yesterday you do not understand the first thing about my type of woman."

"She is tall, dark-haired, and well...we know that she will not have to sing to pay for her supper with a figure like hers."

The prim note in her voice had him laughing. "Oh, that is rich."

"What do you mean?"

"You attend the musicale with a dress you should not be wearing, have men fairly drooling on you, and you have the right to pass judgment on the soprano?"

"They were not drooling over me because of my dress or my looks. Men in that realm do not find women like me all that attractive. That is something I learned years ago, so you will not make a fool out of me pretending that is why they were watching me."

He could not think of a thing to say. At first he was convinced that she was joking with him, but he had heard the pain in her voice. Did Anna actually think that men did not find her desirable?

He studied her bent head as she studied her hands. He knew that her association with Dewhurst had done some damage. Her behavior after the incident that exposed him as a killer, and a man who was using Anna to get to her cousin. But how could this woman who left hundreds of hearts strewn over the ballrooms of London actually believe she had nothing to offer a man but her name and money?

"Anna?"

"Oh, let it go, Daniel. I do not wish to further embarrass myself." He heard it there in her voice, the shame.

"Truly, you cannot think the only reason men are interested in you is your fortune?"

She refused to look at him. It was as the day before. He could not stand being shrugged away as an afterthought, as if he did not matter. He slipped his finger beneath her chin and raised her face until he could see her eyes. What he saw broke his heart.

Tears shimmered in the depths of her blue gaze. The pain and sadness twisted his gut. She tried to pull away but he easily held her still.

"You have to know there is not a man in that crowd who would not be lucky to have you as his wife. Those men might have other motives for any proposal, but I can assure they are all readily attracted to you."

She closed her eyes, causing tears to stream down her cheeks. This was not the girl he knew, the one who was always the life of the party. She had never wanted for attention from the time she was born until the time she was introduced to society. Being a wealthy earl's sister helped, but there was vivacity to her. She lightened every room, drew every eye, and she thought she wasn't the type of woman who attracted men.

It was then he realized that every smile she offered, even her laughter, did not have the same light quality as a few years ago. Sorrow tinged the edges.

"Anna."

She shook her head. "Please, Daniel, let it go." The request came out in a ragged plea. She did not know what that tone in her voice did to him. It shredded what little control he had left.

Keeping her chin firmly in his grasp, he leaned forward and brushed his mouth over hers. She gasped, her eyes opening in surprise. In the next instant, they narrowed.

"If you have any respect for me, please, don't take pity on me. It is one thing I could not stand right now."

"My dear woman, pity is the furthest thing from my mind."

With that, he swooped back down and lost himself in the kiss.

Chapter Nine

For a moment, every thought in Anna's mind dissolved except for one. Daniel was kissing her. His mouth firmly moved over hers, his breath feathered over her skin. In the next instant she felt his tongue glide over her lips. The intimacy of the contact caused her to gasp again. He took full advantage of her parted lips and slipped his tongue inside.

Warmth spiraled through her veins, her head spun. He cupped her face as he slanted his mouth over hers, taking complete and absolute possession. She stopped resisting and just allowed herself to feel. His gloved hands were warm against her flesh, his mouth hot, wet. She could taste the brandy he had drunk earlier. She mimicked his movements by slipping her tongue into his mouth, along his. He groaned and pulled her against him. The heat of him was just amazing. It seeped through her clothes, warmed her. But it was not enough. She needed to be closer, needed to feel his body next to hers.

Without breaking the kiss, he pulled her onto his lap. He balanced her weight with one hand at her back. He slid the other down to cup her breast. His fingers moved over her nipple. It tightened painfully.

She should be shocked to her toes, but she could not seem to gather the thoughts to do so. His fingers glided over the sheer fabric of her bodice and she was lost. She arched against his hand as he continued to kiss her. She did not even protest when he tugged on the delicate fabric and her breast sprang free.

Cold air rushed over her skin, but the next moment, his hand slipped over it. He enticed her, his tongue calling to her, sending waves of heat sparking through her entire body. He continued to seduce her as his fingers moved over her nipple, teasing her. Heat gathered low in her belly and tugged at something she knew had to be lust.

When he tore his mouth away, she opened her mouth to protest, but it ended on a moan as he set his mouth to the column of her neck. As he kissed his way down, she felt the nip of his teeth, the flat of his tongue against her pulse. But he did not stop there. He leaned her back as he continued his way down until he replaced his hand with his mouth.

Shocked and more than a little embarrassed, she pressed her hands against his shoulders but soon found herself slipping her fingers through his hair and urging him on. He moved his tongue over the tip of her nipple, the scrape of his teeth...

She needed to stop this before both of them regretted it. In the next instant, she shivered as he sucked the entire nipple into his mouth.

"Danny."

He lifted his head and looked at her. The heat in his eyes sent a shiver of panic through her. It was too much, almost too overwhelming.

"Say it." His tone dripped with desire.

She shifted on his lap as her most secret of places dampened, throbbed.

"Say what?"

"My name, say it again. Just like you did."

She drew in a deep breath. "Danny."

His eyes grew more intense, the rigid lines in his face more distinct.

He practically growled as he pulled down the rest of her top and bared her other breast. Without preamble, he set about driving her mad in the same manner. Warmth rolled through her, over her nerve endings. Everything that had gathered in her stomach tightened, then dropped between her legs. The pressure caused her to shift again on his lap. This time she felt his hardened manhood against her hip. She stilled as he groaned. Embarrassed, she felt another kind of heat fill her face.

"Oh, Danny, I'm sorry if I hurt you."

He looked at her, a wry smile playing about his lips. The look made him look years younger.

"Anna, you didn't hurt me." He took her face in his hands and drew her near. The molten gold in his eyes shined with admiration and honesty. "You destroyed me."

The utter surrender in his voice made her heart turn over. "Danny."

"Shhh." This time when he kissed her, it was gentle, almost loving. Her throat closed up at the tender look in his eyes. By the time he pulled back, he was not the only one destroyed.

"We are almost there."

It was then she realized they were in a carriage riding through the crowded London streets. In the next instant, she remembered she was sitting there bare-chested.

"Oh my goodness."

She pulled the front of her dress up, her mind still reeling with what had just transpired. She had almost let a rake, a well-known rake at that, seduce her on her way home. In fact, she was not positive if they had been farther from her home that he would not have done just that.

He lifted her off his lap and set her down on the seat opposite his. Even in the dim carriage, she could see him grimace as he shifted in his own seat.

"Are you sure I did not hurt you?"

He chuckled. "No. And I am sure there is no doubt in your mind that men cannot find you desirable."

Cold replaced the heat of their embrace. Embarrassment followed at her naivety. How could she have fallen for such a charade?

"So it was all for show?" She could not keep the pain out of her voice when she asked the question.

The coach shuddered to a stop and he narrowed his gaze on her. "Understand this. I might have done that to prove a point, but it was not all for show. In fact, you are bloody lucky we were not farther from your house. There is a good chance you would not have escaped with your virtue."

Since she had thought the same thing only moments earlier, she decided to keep mum. Her head was still spinning from the kiss, from her speculation on just why he was down in White Chapel the night before. If there was one thing she had learned from her years in society, it was the advantage of a strategic retreat.

She patted her hair. "How do I look?"

He studied her for a second. "Like you have been thoroughly kissed."

She decided to ignore that. The door opened and she pulled her cloak closed as Daniel stepped down in front of her and offered her his hand. She hesitated, afraid to touch him. Truly, she was not sure she would not pull him back in the coach and ask for more. From the surly look he tossed her way, he was not in the mood for that.

She took his hand as she stepped down the carriage. The footman paid her no heed as she walked past him and up the stairs to the front door. Before they could drop the knocker, it opened, revealing her brother.

"Where's Mother?"

For a second, she could not think. Where was her mother? It seemed that Daniel had turned her mind to mush with just a kiss.

"Your mother and mine went to the Fillmores' ball," Daniel said.

Sebastian looked at Daniel, then her, then back to Daniel. "Then I thank you for bringing Anna home safely."

His tone had turned icy as he continued to stare at Daniel. Oh, bother, her brother must be able to tell. Her face flushed as they continued to stare at each other.

"Really, Sebastian, are you trying to freeze me to death." She used the same tone her mother used to scare both of them while they were growing up. Sebastian snapped out of it and stepped out of her way.

"Good night, Anna."

She turned and smiled at Daniel. "Thank you for bringing me home."

She stepped inside and waited for Sebastian to shut the door. He hesitated and then shut the door.

"Anna?"

She sighed, thinking she had been close to freedom. "Yes?"

"Did anything happen in the carriage that I should know about?"

Her heart stuttered and she had to gather her thoughts. When she turned to face him, she made sure to keep her expression as calm as possible.

"What do you mean?"

For the first time in years, she witnessed her brother blush. "It is just...well, your..." He gestured toward her face.

"Yes?"

"Well, you look like you have been kissed."

He said it with so much disgust she thought it might have

sickened him to even think of his sister being kissed. The former rake apparently did not want to accept that she was a woman.

She laughed. "And who would have done the kissing? Daniel? A man who I think of as a brother? I am sure he has never seen me as more than a sister. I am hardly Daniel's type even if I did have a *tendre* for him."

He shoved his hands into the pockets of his trousers and rocked back on his heels as he studied her. "You assure me nothing happened?"

She cast her eyes toward the heavens and turned around to head up the stairs. "I told you nothing happened. I have an early morning so I am off to bed."

Daniel came awake with a start, knowing that someone was in his room—again. There was very little chance it was anyone dangerous because getting into his home was downright impossible. But he continued to lie there as he barely opened his eyes. The first streams of light filtered through the drapery, telling him it was at least ten in the morning. From the way the person walked, he knew exactly who it was.

"Does Colleen know you sneak around men's bedrooms? I knew she was forward thinking, but this peculiar habit is beyond that."

"Bloody hell. You always know it's me."

He rolled over and squinted at Sebastian. "What are you doing here?"

"I wanted to talk to you about last night."

Daniel wanted nothing more than to groan and pull the covers up over his head. He still could not believe he lost so much control with Anna. He could not bear to see the pain in her eyes, hear it in her voice. He had planned to just kiss that pain away. He should have known better. The moment he had touched her, he had lost every sane thought in his head. And he had paid for it. What little sleep he had gotten had been filled with images of Anna beneath him, those same blue eyes shimmering with need as he rode her to completion.

He suppressed a groan and raised his leg. He didn't want to explain just why he had a full cock stand to his best friend. "What actually did you want to discuss?"

"My sister."

"There is nothing to discuss."

"So she said. But I know what she looked like."

"And how is that?" Daniel asked, keeping his voice as steady as possible.

Sebastian studied him for a second, crossing his arms over his chest. "Like she had been kissed."

"I did not touch your sister. Good God, man, I think of her as one of my sisters."

He said that lie without blinking. There would be no way he could ever put her in that category again. Not when he knew just how soft her lips were, the way her breast felt beneath his hand. By God she had responded readily. To think she thought herself undesirable to men. He would have given anything in the world to strip her down, lay her on his bed and do his best to convince her just how desirable she is.

Sebastian stared him for a second to two, but Daniel kept his face expressionless.

Finally, his friend relented. He settled on the bed and looked at Daniel's chest. "All right, I will believe you, this time. I see my sister looking like that again after being in your presence and I will not hesitate to throttle you. Now that I have cleared that up, what the bloody hell have you been doing to yourself? Is that a knife wound?"

Inwardly, he cursed. Keeping his secret duty from Sebastian was one of the hardest chores. Sebastian was no one's fool, and there'd been times Daniel was sure his best friend suspected something.

"Just a little trouble, trying to help a friend out."

He raised one eyebrow. "I understand there are things you have not told me." Daniel opened his mouth but Sebastian held his hand up. "No. Don't try and lie to me. I told you last night that I've known you too long. I know when you are lying. But there is one thing you need to understand. I will stand up for you, protect you against any enemy."

He did not know what to say to that. Daniel had always known that Sebastian was honorable, knew that in most cases he could count on him for support. From the tone in his friend's voice, he understood that whatever Daniel would not share with him was dangerous. But Daniel knew without a doubt Sebastian would do anything to protect him.

"But if whatever has caused you these injuries even gets close to my sister, I will kill you myself."

Daniel nodded, but said nothing else as the serious expression dissolved from Sebastian's face.

"Now, get your arse out of bed and get dressed. I am going to be a father again and you need to congratulate me."

That afternoon, Daniel looked up from the estate's accounts to see Jo striding into his library unannounced. He scowled at her. He was still in a foul mood, not fit company for any woman.

"What are you doing here?"

The smile she shot him had little heat. "Don't you have a kiss for your Aunty?"

"Stop it, Jo. What is the matter?"

Her face lost its jovial expression. She drew in a breath as she collapsed in one of the chairs. "There seems to be people making inquiries about Lady Anna."

An icy finger traced down his spine. "Who?"

"I am not sure. I just know there have been some strangers asking about her around the area. One of the store keepers sent word to Jack."

"Dammit!" He jumped out of his chair and began to pace. "Just what the bloody hell do I do now?"

"I would suggest you stay as close as possible."

He tossed her a look and continued his pacing. "That would make her more of a target. On top of that, I was practically warned off by her brother today."

Jo's golden brown eyes widened. "Sebastian? Why would he do that?"

The memories of the night before in the carriage tumbled forward in his mind. Jesus, he didn't think there would ever be a day he would forget the way her mouth tasted or the way her flesh felt beneath his fingers. He could still hear those little sighs and mewls. He had not lied to her. He knew without a doubt with thirty more minutes in that carriage, he would have had her virginity.

"Ahhh," Jo said.

His face heated. "What do you mean by that?"

She smiled. "It is easy to figure out just what that look on your face meant."

"I think of her as a sister."

"If you look like that thinking about her, you do not think of her as a sister."

He waved that away, not in the mood to get in an argument that would take valuable time.

"Sebastian came by this morning. He told me to stay away."

She frowned. "Truly? I thought he was your best friend."

"He is, but he knows what I do is dangerous."

All color left her face. "You have told him what you do?"

He made a face. "No. But Sebastian isn't stupid. He definitely knows I do something."

She nodded. "We have no one else. Simon's in the country at the moment, and everyone else I have who would be good at this would not be able to move about in her circles."

He ground his teeth. "It cannot be me."

"You can hover."

He could not. He knew the moment that he witnessed another man asking her for a waltz, there would be no way he could keep from beating the man senseless. Beside that fact, being close to her meant he had to touch her. Knowing that she had wanted him, had been more than willing to go further than they did last night, was going to drive him mad. It made the itch he had for her intensify.

"You have to, Daniel. There is no other way."

Knowing he was defeated, he sighed and nodded.

"I must be going. Jack is spending time around the orphanage today, keeping an eye out there."

"Her brother has hired some muscle for that."

Jo smiled wryly. "Jack doesn't trust them. He wants to see to it himself. It seems that Lady Anna impressed him quite a bit the other night."

He thought of her cool headedness in the situation. Most women of her station would have fainted. Anna had called out orders as if she were a general.

"She tends to take charge."

Jo nodded. "Oh, and was there a reason you did not tell me of the Viper returning?"

The arched eyebrow meant he was in trouble. It was hard to figure a woman like Jo, several years younger than himself, could order him about. But then his uncle had trained her well.

"I did not want to worry anyone."

"I know that you might be used to leaving the women out of it, but just so you understand, this is my job. I might not be the one in command, but I am your associate."

He could tell by the tone in her voice that she had been hurt. "I apologize. I wanted to investigate it before I told anyone. I thought it might not be real."

"I put Bart on it. He will see if there have been any more incidences. Your father was not the only one he targeted years ago."

That caught his attention."He wasn't?"

"No. There were several men targeted. Even Harold got letters, but nothing happened to him."

"Tell Jack I will get someone to handle the nighttime watch."

She smiled. "I will, but I am not that sure he will allow it. He seems very protective of Lady Anna."

She slipped out of the library, leaving him alone with his thoughts. He looked out upon the street, saw people go about their daily business and wondered just where the Viper resided? He was of their class, that much his father had discovered before his death. They had thought the man dead, or possibly run to the continent to escape scrutiny. Why now? It made no sense whatsoever.

And to target Anna? For what reason? He knew that their families were well known to be friends, but why would he even think to target her? Unless Daniel had been watched the entire time.

Another shiver of dread circled in his stomach. Of course, he had been watched. And anyone watching saw them leave together. Viper had to know that Daniel had shown some interest.

He still wanted to stay away, but he knew Jo was right. There was no doubt in his mind that even if he pretended not to pay any attention to her, she was now a target. There would be no way to protect her, unless he told her and Sebastian. And that would put the two of them at an even more risk.

"Daniel."

"Yes, Mother, did Jo find you?"

She nodded. "Yes, and she told me what happened. You are going to start coming to more balls?"

"I thought Anna didn't like them."

"Her mother made her agree. After Anna disappeared the night you were attacked, her mother used it to her advantage. If she didn't go, she would not be allowed to spend all her extra time at the orphanage. Victoria wants her married."

Daniel snorted and turned to the street again. "Don't worry, Mother. I will ensure that she is protected."

He heard the swish of her skirts as she approached him. "You must be the one to do it, my dear."

He ground his teeth again. "I said I would to it."

"That's a good boy." She leaned up on her toes and gave him a quick buss on the cheek. "Tonight it is the Fredricks' Ball. I understand that Anna will be attending with only her mother since Colleen is doing poorly."

He smiled and glanced at his mother. "Yes, Sebastian told me the good news this morning."

She looked like she might say something, but Daniel turned back to the window. He did not want to discuss it, did not even want to think about it. How could he? He had always been happy for his best friend and the happiness he had found with Colleen, but now for some reason, Daniel felt a gnawing envy digging into his gut. His mother hesitated but then left him alone.

He had felt horrible that morning trying to smile as he congratulated his best friend on his third child. But it now bothered him. For the first time ever, he wanted to be the one announcing the birth of his child. Never before this week had he wanted to marry and have children. And he knew the reason why.

He closed his eyes and the image of Anna came to his mind. She had looked adorable with her lips reddened from his mouth. No other woman had left him shaking with this overwhelming need with just a kiss. Lord, she was a novice, did not even know what she did to him. It was a good thing she did not. Knowing Anna, she would use it against him.

He opened his eyes. Now he had to spend time with her, around her, and not touch her. What he did for God and country truly went beyond the call of duty.

Chapter Ten

"Can I have this dance?"

Anna stared at Daniel and wondered what he was about. "I…"

There was a stunned silence in the men who surrounded her. She had spent the last three years building the reputation that kept her insulated and off the dance floor. In the last few weeks, Daniel had shredded it. Her standing for only dancing with family had been shredded by Daniel.

As he smiled at her, she knew that he had trapped her on purpose. She could not refuse and he knew it. Declining his request would draw attention to them. Granted, she didn't care, but she knew without a doubt that her mother would. Besides being a friend of the family, Daniel's family line was old and well respected. It would be seen as a slight if she did not dance with him.

"Of course."

She placed her hand on his arm and allowed him to lead her through the crowd. He took her into his arms and swung her into the waltz.

"What are you about?"

He looked down at her then back up over her shoulder again. "I have no idea what you are talking about."

"This. You don't attend balls and you definitely don't ask

me to dance."

"I danced with you several days ago."

"Yes, and it had been years since we have danced. Now you have attended three events that I have been at in less than two weeks." She frowned. "Did my mother put you up to this?"

He started and looked down at her. "Why on earth would your mother want me to ask you to dance?"

"Apparently, she thinks I need to marry, which I disagree with."

He smiled. "So she thinks I should court you?"

"Goodness, never! But my mother probably thinks that your attention will draw the attention of some suitors."

A flash of anger sparked in his gaze before he quickly masked it. He looked away again. "That is stupid."

"Of course it is. I doubt my mother has thought things through. It is not like my mother at all. Scheming is not really what she does."

"What I mean is that it is stupid to think that she needs to scheme. Good Lord, you are an heiress and beyond that, you are the most beautiful woman in the room. Why would you need your mother to scheme to find you a husband?"

The tone in his voice told her he was serious. And for a moment she said nothing as he moved her around the floor. In fact, she was stunned. Did Daniel know just what he had said? From the expression on his face, he might not have. He just took it as fact. And even though she knew it wasn't true, her heart tripped. She knew some people thought her beautiful, but to have Daniel say it meant so much more.

"Be that as it may, there seems to be something on my mother's mind, something that is goading her on. It is truly getting to be a nuisance."

"To think that you need to interest men. Why that preposterous dress you are wearing is bad enough."

The music slowly died down and they came to a stop. "What is wrong with my dress?"

Something seemed to clear from his gaze and he realized where they were. "What I mean is..."

He looked around and realized another dance was starting. He took her arm and worked their way out of the ballroom.

The cool air hit her skin and she breathed a sigh. "I really cannot fathom why I loved balls. It truly is the most uncomfortable experience. So hot."

"How you can even be hot in that dress is beyond me?"

She glanced at him. "Why are you complaining about my dress again? It is designed by Fredricka."

He grunted. "There was apparently a shortage of silk."

She stared at him. "What do you mean?"

"She left the front of it entirely too low—again."

Anger swelled. "It isn't your place, as I told you last time we had this discussion. I am a woman grown and I can choose what to wear."

"Yes, apparently you are. And if you are the one choosing them, why did you choose something so scandalous?"

She looked down at her dress then back up at him. "Just what are you talking about?"

"You leave your wares for all to see. It looks like you agree with your mother."

All the warmth from his earlier comment seeped away. "I am tired of hearing you attack my choice in dresses. I picked it because I liked it. I did not buy it for anyone but myself. I never think of how I will look to men."

He snorted and shot her a look of askance. "Tell me another tale. Women always buy things to gain men's attention."

She threw her hands up in the air. "This is ridiculous."

"I agree."

She crossed her arms beneath her breasts. "Then why are we arguing?"

"I have no idea."

She humphed. "Please take me back inside. I did not even want to come tonight and now you have made it completely unpleasant."

He shot her a look. "I didn't want to come tonight either."

"Then why are you here?"

He looked at her, his gaze direct. He opened his mouth. But nothing came out. It was odd to find Daniel with nothing to say. With his quick wit he was usually ready with a rejoinder.

"My mother begged me. I cannot say no."

That was the truth from what she could discern, but Anna had an idea there was something else there, something that had brought him out. She wished it was her. She wished that their kiss last night had driven him to distraction as it had her.

"We should return." She nodded and allowed him to return her to the stuffy ballroom. As she watched him walk away, she thought not for the first time that it was a pity she could not have the one man she knew would truly make her happy.

Daniel stood as his supervisor at the War Department strode into his study. It was bad enough he showed up without an appointment, but there was a scowl on Sir Alexander's face.

The doors shut almost silently behind him.

"Do you want to explain why you did not tell me that you have been injured?"

It had been over a week since the attack. "I've yet to file my report."

Which was even worse than not sending him information right away about it.

The older gentleman bristled. "You are as bad as your damned father." Since they had been close friends, it was said with some affection. "If your mother had not talked to me about it, I would have never known."

"You talked to my mother. About me? Am I in leading strings?"

"Daniel! I will not allow you to go off running around after this Viper person again if you do not keep me apprised."

Which brought Daniel up short. Sir Alexander was definitely his supervisor, but he tended to allow Daniel to run his group of spies the way he wanted to. Not once in the last five years had he stepped in.

"Understood."

"Now I understand Jo is on this. Your mother mentioned you think it is the same person who killed your father. Why?"

Daniel motioned to the seats in front of his desk as he went to the sideboard for some brandy. He picked up the bottle and waited for Sir Alexander's nod.

As he poured, he talked. "I would think that it would have to be the same man. He knew my father had been targeted, only the Viper knew that. Oh, and you and Mother."

"He was not the only man who had been targeted. There was your uncle too."

"But he is family. This almost seems to be personal."

"You think the man isn't even a spy?"

"I would not say that. The setup the night I was stabbed spoke of a man who was accustomed with elaborate schemes. Definitely had the mark of a spy."

"But for some reason this turned personal?"

"Yes. And for that, I need my father's records. I need to look over anything that happened during his time as a spy."

Sir Alexander nodded as he sipped his brandy. "There is a

worse situation if it isn't the same man."

Daniel nodded. "Yes. If it isn't the same man, that means he has knowledge of the former spy. And that means he is either within our circle, or very close to someone in our circle. There is also a possibility that he is a protégé, someone our last Viper trained."

"Damned man."

"I tend to agree with you. And I hope to send the bastard to hell."

Anna arrived on time to the orphanage when a man caught her eye. She slowed her movements of opening the door so she could study him out of the corner of her eye. His hunched appearance, his cap...he looked like a hundred other day laborers in the area. But it took another moment of study before she placed him. She hurried down the steps and was gratified to see his eyes widen.

"You're Daniel's man Jack." She could not keep the accusation out of her voice.

"Yes. Sometimes."

"What does that mean? And just what in heavens are you doing skulking around here? You aren't looking for another loan shark are you?"

"No, miss. I mean, my lady. I heard that you had some trouble. I wanted to make sure that nothing was going on?"

"Trouble."

"Someone trying to break in the other night."

"Oh." That had some of her temper dissolving. "You promise that Lord Bridgerton didn't send you here to spy on me."

His face reddened and she thought she had him. He pulled off his hat and then said, "No, my lady. I just wanted to make sure that no one was bothering you."

She sighed and crossed her arms. "Well, come on."

His eyes widened. "What?"

"I cannot leave you out here in this rain. Come in. I am sure there are a few hot buns still left."

She turned and started back up the steps again. When she didn't hear him follow her, she looked back over her shoulder. He was standing in the same place he had been before, a strange look on his face.

"Well, come on...Jack? Right?"

He nodded and moved to walk behind her. She unlocked the door and stepped inside. Instantly, the warmth of the hall filled her. She had not realized just how cold she was. Jack closed the door behind him.

"I do not think this is proper."

She glanced at him. "First, I did not ask. Second, you cannot think that I would leave you out there."

Before he could respond, Mrs. Markham came bustling up. "Oh, you do look cold. Who is this?"

"He is apparently my guard. He is a friend of Lord Bridgerton and heard of the attempted break in. The two beefy guards—yes, I did see them outside—are not enough apparently."

"Oh, no worries on that account. That is what I was hurrying down to tell you. We discovered the person trying to break in was just that Carlotta woman."

"The...uh...working woman I talked to?"

"Yes. She wanted to see you, wanted to take you up on your offer."

Relief filled her. Not only because the break-in had been nothing, but also because it seemed she had reached another of those poor women. "That is stupendous."

She smiled at her new friend. "So you can see that I do not need anyone here to watch me."

He frowned, but said nothing.

"I promised Jack some hot buns. I am sure a spot of tea will warm him right up."

As Mrs. Markham bustled Jack in the direction of the kitchen, Anna went in search of their newly acquired resident. They did not always house women in the orphanage, and they were very careful to keep them separate from the children. The truth of the matter was she could not trust them. Some devious women would come to the orphanage to gain the boys' acceptance and then lure them away into thievery or worse, prostitution. While it was hard to imagine, she had known it to happen elsewhere and Anna refused to allow anyone to hurt her children.

She was a bit breathless as she gained the third floor. These nights out were going to be the death of her. She could not keep attending balls and musicales to the early morning, then work all day at the orphanage.

When she came into the room, a lone woman sat on the bed looking outside. Carlotta was a beautiful woman. Beautiful long black curls dripped over her shoulders, and Anna knew without seeing them that her hazel eyes were more green than brown. She was small in stature, like a porcelain doll. There had to be some Spanish in her background. She spoke it fluently, without a hint of English accent.

Anna moved into the room and Carlotta turned to look at her. The black eye she sported almost made Anna gasp. To think someone had felt the need to hit this slight woman disgusted her.

She turned and curtsied, making Anna think, not for the first time, that she came from impoverished gentry. "My lady."

Carlotta grimaced when she rose. Anna rushed forward.

"Are you all right?"

She nodded but she sat on the small cot. "Just a few bruises, my lady."

Anna sat on the cot opposite of her. "Mrs. Markham told me that you were the one trying to get in the other night."

She nodded and looked out the window.

"Did you get hurt then?"

Carlotta nodded again.

Anna moved to place her hand over hers, but the woman started. Fear had her eyes going wide. Stifling the regret that such a young woman would fear even the smallest of touches, Anna sat back.

"Doctor Timms will be here to see you later today."

"What for?"

"To make sure you aren't hurt worse than you appear."

"Then?"

"Then you will rest. After you are healed, we will discuss what you will do with your future."

She glanced at Anna and a look of pure need flashed in the woman's eyes. It struck her as hard as any physical blow. These poor women went without love, without acceptance, without even the simple touch to assure them they were worthy of affection.

"I will leave you to rest. Mrs. Markham will bring the doctor up here later, but she will stay here if you want her to during the examination."

"Yes, my lady. But...what shall I do to earn my keep?"

"We will figure that out all in time." She stood. "I wish we had known you were trying to get in when you came to our door."

Carlotta frowned. "I would have been back sooner, but there was a man skulking about."

That caught Anna's attention. "A man? One of the guards out front?"

"No, m'lady. He was hanging around across the street, in the alley. I thought it might be someone I was trying to avoid."

Anna wanted to ask the young woman who, but the closed expression on her face told her she would not reveal the name. Probably the man who beat her.

Anna nodded. "Please, rest. I have work to do, but I will check back in later."

Mutely, the woman nodded and looked back out the window again. Anna sighed and then started back down to the first floor. She ignored the clamor of feet, the raised voices, the laughter as thoughts about their newest resident and what she had revealed turned over in her head. Anna did not like the idea of someone watching the orphanage. The fact that neither of the guards had noticed was a bit disturbing. She would definitely mention it to Sebastian so he could talk to the guards.

That decided, her thoughts turned back to Carlotta and the women like her. As she reached her office, she decided to come up with some kind of outreach, some network where the girls could gain their attention. She did not want to think of another woman left out in the cold. They needed to know where to come if they needed help.

With her mind set, she strode into her office and decided to set things in motion.

Anna looked out over the lawn of the Greenwood household and thought not for the first time that this was a waste of time. She knew why her mother had wanted her to attend. She desperately wanted Anna to find a match, but it was not to be. It never would be. After her kiss a few nights before, she knew there would never be another man who would even be able to compare to Daniel. She had been kissed before. But not one of her suitors had been able to take her mind along with her. It had been the first time in her life she had lost complete control. Oh, she had lost her head over Dewhurst when he promised her romance and plotted to kill her cousin. But there had never been a time she had been so willing to allow a man to compromise her.

She closed her eyes and leaned her forehead against the cool window pane. It had been a long few days readying for the trip. The one ball she had attended before their departure had been exquisite torture. That just would not do. She could not lose her composure around him again. It was bad enough that he knew she was attracted to him. No woman kissed a man the way she had if she was not. She had to learn to control herself around him. She had dreaded this trip, but maybe it was a good thing. Now she could definitely use the time away from her nemesis to regroup. Once she could keep herself controlled around him, she could ferret out what was going on with him. Inquiries to Sebastian had definitely gotten her nowhere. In fact, he had warned her away from Daniel. Decidedly odd.

She opened her eyes and looked down at the next carriage that rolled into view. She knew Lady Adelaide had planned to attend, but when the door opened, it was not the woman she saw, but rather her son.

Oh, Lord in heaven. What had she done to deserve this? She watched as he looked at the surroundings, taking in the hustle and bustle. Then, as if he knew exactly where she was, he looked up at her window. She stilled, her whole body going hot under his gaze. Her breasts ached, her body yearned. The smile that curled his lips was just a little too self-satisfied for her tastes. How could he see how he affected her?

With a jaunty salute, he turned to help his mother down from the carriage. Needing to regroup, she moved away. What had she been thinking to stand there and stare at him as if she were some mooncalf in love? And just what the devil was he doing at this party? It was definitely not his type of thing. Tame by his standards. Did it have to do with the mysterious stabbing? What if he owed someone money...could he be forced to hide in the country?

She rolled the idea over in her mind but got nowhere. She would just have to ask around to discover his motives for being at the country party. Because she could not allow him into her heart. Years ago, she had done that. Her girlhood fascination with the man had almost killed her when she'd arrived in town to find their relationship changed. Anna knew if she allowed him to capture her this time, she would never recover.

Chapter Eleven

Daniel glanced around the library and sighed with relief. No matchmaking mamas were hiding in the shadows. It had been horrible since he had arrived at the party earlier in the day. Women had been thrown at him left and right. It seemed that his attendance had made everyone think he was here to find a wife.

He closed the door behind him and walked to the couch. He could not even disappear to his room. The last time he tried that, he had been accosted by Lady Fontemain who offered her daughter up on a silver platter. Along with the fringe benefits her mother could offer. It had left him feeling slightly sick and in need of a bath. He knew he was jaded, but he had never seen something so disgusting as a woman pimping herself to get her daughter married.

He moved to sit down and encountered legs and a squeak.

"What on earth are you doing?"

He looked down and found the woman he had been ordered—by his mother and Jack—to protect for the weekend. Anna was in delightful dishabille, her hair slightly mussed, her dressed wrinkled.

"I could ask you the same thing."

She pulled herself up to a sitting position and swung her legs to the ground. "I am taking a rest."

He crossed his arms and lifted one eyebrow.

"All right. I was hiding. I cannot seem to avoid anyone, even in my room."

"I know the feeling," he murmured.

She eyed him. "Someone accosted you in your room?"

His blood ran cold as he thought of what might have happened to her. "There was a man in your room?"

She rolled her eyes. "No. Lady Reynolds called on me. Just why do people behave differently at house parties?"

Despite the situation, he smiled. He could not help it. She sounded so indignant. "I have no idea."

She humphed. "So I picked the one place that I thought the woman would not come into."

"Really, the library?"

"There are books here. She avoids anything where she might learn."

He couldn't stop the laugh that burst out of him. "You definitely know the woman."

She narrowed her gaze on him. "What are you doing here?"

He thought of his encounter and frowned. "I had the same problem, only with another mother."

"Hmm. That would be interesting to find out who that was, but knowing you, you will not tell me. What I meant is what are you doing at this party?"

For a second, he couldn't think of anything to say. He knew that his mother had given him a story, one about looking for a wife or some such idiocy, but he couldn't remember really how to speak.

"Daniel."

He shook himself. "I think that would be obvious."

She cocked her head to one side. "No, it truly isn't."

He cleared his throat and settled onto the couch on the

opposite end. "I am here to find a wife."

If anything, her face lost all expression. "Oh."

"Mother thinks it is time to find one, and I daresay I think she is right. I am getting up there in years."

She frowned. "Your mother asked you to do this and you decided to come to find a wife?"

He nodded.

"You're lying."

He kept his expression blank as he said nothing.

"Really, Daniel, if you are going to lie, you need to be better at it."

That took him back. He was well known to be the best bluffer of the group, able to lie to just about anyone. The fact that she saw through it was disturbing and arousing.

"That is the reason I am here. Much for the same reason your mother has dragged you here."

She sighed. "Very well." She rose and started toward the door. "But, Daniel, you might want to be a little more active in finding a wife. Hiding in the library isn't the best place to find one."

And with that, she slipped out the door and left him alone to his thoughts. Really, the woman was a menace to his sanity. Even just being in her presence for several minutes he wanted her. He ached to touch her, to strip off the pink confection she was wearing and explore every bit of flesh it exposed. He closed his eyes and asked for guidance, but the only thing he could hear was the way his name had sounded on her lips.

Anna watched Daniel from the shadows as he walked around the room. She had never really noticed it before, but now that she studied him, she knew that he was looking for something or someone. Her heart sank as she thought about their conversation before. Even knowing he was lying to her, it had hurt to hear him say the words. He paused to talk to his mother and she noticed that he continued his survey. This went beyond just watching others. There was something almost...military in his behavior.

"You won't find a man back here, Lady Anna."

She jumped at the sound of the low, female voice. Lady Joanna stepped up beside her. "That is why you are here."

Anna turned back around. "That is why my mother wants me to be here."

Lady Joanna laughed. "Yes, I can see that. Your mother is ready to have you settled."

The knowing tone in the other woman's voice irritated Anna. She could not help gnashing her teeth together.

"I thought you did not like such amusements, Lady Joanna."

"I do not, probably not any more than you do. But duty calls."

Anna cut her a look and noticed that she too was watching Daniel. Jealousy surged through her as Lady Joanna turned to look at her with a knowing look on her face.

"So you have come for assignations." Just saying it hurt.

Joanna shook her head. "Don't believe everything you see or hear, Lady Anna."

Anna opened her mouth to ask her a question but she said, "And do not believe Daniel either. He is...too smart for his own good." She looked at Anna, her expression serious for the first time. "He is entirely too stupid when it comes to you."

"I need to get back to my room. It is just too stifling in here."

Joanna moved out the French doors to the left of them.

Before she could discern just what the older woman had meant, Daniel was standing in front of her.

"What the devil are you doing here?" Daniel asked.

"Hiding."

That took him back. "I have been looking for you."

So it had been her he had been looking around the room for. Interesting. "And here I am. You can go away now."

"Your mother is not going to be happy with you if you do not even dance."

"I am not in the mood." She was irritated beyond belief at her mother. What on earth had possessed her seemingly intelligent mother to tell people Anna was looking for a husband? And rumors were swirling about her fortune. Every fortune hunter in attendance had been bothering her. This had been the one place she could hide.

"Come now, the waltz is next I believe."

She gave him a suspicious glare. She truly loved to waltz and it had been one of the things she had missed the most the past few years. But she would not expose herself to the hordes of suitors.

"No, thank you."

He sighed. "Anna, you cannot hide here all night."

"I can at least for a while." She hated the idea that her voice rose like a little girl's. "It is the only course of action that makes sense."

He eyed her suspiciously. "What is the matter?"

She hesitated. "My mother has told people I am looking for a husband."

"That is what most people are presuming."

"And that I have a bigger fortune than people previously thought."

His eyes widened. "Good God, what was she thinking?"

She nodded. "Every fortune hunter in attendance has been bothering me. Including that creepy Lord Seaton."

"Lord Seaton? He is older than your mother!"

"Shhh. You will draw attention to us." She looked around but was happy to realize that Daniel had not been heard.

"Your mother must have lost her mind. Does Sebastian know about this?"

She shook her head. "I just found out myself. I really do not know what my mother is thinking."

He crossed his arms over his massive chest and glared. "To lie like this is just not her usual thing."

"She knows I do not want to marry." Anna sighed. "So here I hide. And it is a shame because I do like to waltz."

He smiled and grabbed her hand. "Come."

Before she could say anything, he pulled her through the doors and away from the heat of the dance.

When they were free of the others, he released her hand. She smiled.

"This is getting to be a habit with us."

"What?" he said as he looked around as if looking for something.

"Being alone, out on the terrace."

He frowned at her. "I did it so that we could dance."

He took her hand again and drew her into the shadows. Then he drew her into his arms. Without the ballroom full of people watching them, he drew her closer, so close she could feel the heat of his body. When she took a deep breath, her breasts brushed against his chest.

He moved her around the terrace, just as he had before on the dance floor, all power and grace, but this was more intimate. It was only the two of them, dancing in the shadows.

She looked up at him and found his serious gaze. She

could not look away. Something shifted in his eyes, something so dark it should have frightened her, but it did not. Instead, she felt a jolt of awareness swiftly followed by a rush of excitement.

He continued the dance, his gaze never wavering from hers. She thought it impossible but he pulled her closer. The scent of him filled her senses. Bayberry, musky, so much Daniel as she knew him.

Before she was ready, the dance was over, but he did not release her. He stopped dancing and she felt his hand move over her back.

"Daniel?"

She could barely hear her own voice over the country reel that had started inside. She knew that soon they would be missed, that someone, probably her mother, would come looking for her at some point. But she could not seem to get herself to tell him they needed to return.

"You called me something else the other night." His voice was deep, resonate. It sent a shiver of heat lancing through her veins.

"What?"

"In the carriage. You called me Danny."

She closed her eyes as the images from that night came rushing back to the forefront of her mind. In her weakest moment, she had called him that. It was the name that she had always called him in her mind. Danny, her friend, her playmate. She opened her eyes and realized that this was not her playmate, the man she'd grown to love. This was someone else, darker, more dangerous.

She swallowed. "I know, but that was a mistake."

His golden brown gaze searched hers. "Do you really believe that?"

She wanted to say yes. It was the smart thing to say, to

132

believe. The other path would lead her to ruin. But she knew in her heart that it was not what she wanted, needed.

"No."

Something passed over his expression, something dark and forbidden. He tugged her out of the shadows, but instead of going back to the ballroom, he pulled her down the steps and into the garden. The air was extremely cool, but she wasn't cold at all. Instead, her entire body shivered with excitement.

He led her to the far end of the garden to a folly. He opened the door, stuck his head inside and then pulled her behind him as he strode into it.

Before she could ask him what was going on, he pulled her into his arms and started kissing her. He did not give her time to think, to even form an opinion of what was happening. He just took her mouth and plunged her into the heated pleasure of his kiss.

Daniel knew what he was doing, knew it was wrong, but he could not help it. All he had wanted was to keep her safe and happy. He had known that she loved to dance, especially the waltz. Knowing that she was hiding out and missing one of her true pleasures, he could not stand by and allow her to miss out.

He took her face into his hands and deepened the kiss, slipped his tongue into her mouth. God, the taste of her was beyond anything he had ever known. That there would never be another woman who tasted like this enticed him without even knowing it.

She moaned against his tongue, the vibrations shivering through his entire body. He walked her backwards to a couch against the back wall. Breaking the kiss, he sat and then pulled Anna down onto it next to him.

"Danny—"

He did not give her time to respond. Instead, he took her

again, leaning over her, using his extra weight to press his point. She hesitated for a moment. But in the next second, she dove into the kiss with him, thrusting her tongue against his. Excitement flowered, expanded. He knew what he was doing was wrong, was against everything he knew he should be doing. But at the moment, he could not get his mind to work. All he could think of was Anna.

He made quick work of her dress. One tug and her breasts were exposed to his view. Anna gasped. The breathless sound was one of the most erotic things he had heard in his life. But he could not pause to tell her or even contemplate that.

The moonlight in the folly gave him a better view than he had the night in the carriage. Alabaster ivory, tipped with rosebuds. He skimmed the back of his fingers over each breast, delighted when she shivered.

He looked up at her and smiled at the blush now darkening her cheeks. She was a pleasure to behold. Without breaking eye contact, he bent his head over her breast and drew one sweet nipple into his mouth. Another gasp, but he ignored it and closed his eyes. Soon, the tender bud had tightened and her hands were now clenched in his hair.

Everything in him ached to take her, to make her his, but he knew that it would not be possible. But he could give her relief. He eased her on her back, then slid his hand down her body. As he continued to taste, tease and drive them both out of their minds, he eased her skirts up and stole beneath. He skimmed her hands up her thighs to the soft curls that lay at the top shielding her sweet honey pot. He eased his way up, placing a hand on each of her thighs, and touched his mouth to her very core.

"Danny!"

She tried to sit up and shove her skirts down. He ignored her. He slipped his tongue inside, sighing with pleasure as the taste of her exploded through his senses. Her protests turned to moans as he delved into her honey pot again and again. Her legs shifted restlessly beside his head, her hands molding to the back of his head.

He pulled back and could not help but smile when she protested. He replaced his mouth with his hand, slipping his finger inside. Her muscles clamped down on his digit as he pressed his thumb against the tight bud, pushing her up and over the edge. Her mouth opened on a silent cry. Her orgasm shimmered through her body as she bowed. His heart constricted at the sight. God, she was beautiful.

Every part of his being told him to take her, to slip inside her snug core and ride her into another orgasm. He wanted to claim her, make her his. But before he could get his mind to function, he heard a twig snap just outside the door. It was enough to pull him out of his thoughts and into action. He sat and pulled Anna up off the couch. The smile curving her lips told him all he needed to know. Daniel could not resist the quick kiss.

"I think there is someone here, love."

"Daniel?"

He ignored her, only saying, "Fix your dress."

She gasped as she looked down and pulled up her dress. The door creaked open, causing Daniel to pull them into a darkened area behind a statue.

"I know you are in here, Daniel. Come out now."

Chapter Twelve

Anna's heart came to a stuttering stop the moment she recognized Lady Joanna's voice. Oh, this was horrible. She did not want to ever be caught in such a situation but definitely not by the woman who was Daniel's previous paramour.

"Jo, you have a really bad timing."

"I hate to bother you, but we have a problem." Lady Joanna's voice lashed out at Anna. Her embarrassment grew. She would not be amazed if her whole body was blushing.

He stepped in front of Anna to shield her from Lady Joanna's line of vision. "Go back to the house, I will meet you there."

Anna blinked at Daniel's tone. This was not the lover she had been with just moments before. There was a ring of authority she had never heard before in it.

"You don't seem to realize the problem. Lady Anna's absence has been noted. As has yours."

Daniel muttered something beneath his breath then turned to her. "We need to get you back to the house as inconspicuously as possible."

She glanced over his shoulder at Lady Joanna. "Did anyone see you in the area?"

Lady Joanna shook her head. "No. It was Jack who told me what was going on."

Anna smiled as she turned her attention back to Daniel. "This will be easy. Lady Joanna and I will return to the party. We will come up with something to say we were talking about." An idea formed. "I can say I was trying to get money for the orphanage."

Daniel frowned and opened his mouth but Lady Joanna jumped in. "That is a wonderful idea. You can return later, say you were somewhere else, smoking or something."

She had drawn even with Daniel and reached out to Anna with her hand, pulling her along. "Come, let's return. I do think your mother was seriously worried."

Anna sighed. "Mother has become such a worrier of late."

"Anna," Daniel said. She paused and he gave Lady Joanna a look that would scare most men. The other woman humphed.

"I will be waiting outside."

Once she left them alone, Daniel hesitated, then took her hand. All the sudden, the folly seemed smaller, almost as if the walls were closing in on her. Even as her body warmed under his study, a chill slipped down her spine.

He played with her fingers. "I did not plan for something like this to happen. I will speak to your mother in the morning."

Mortification slashed at her. She knew without a doubt that Daniel did not love her. He had been carried away in the moment, just as she had. Yes, she loved him. She had compared every man she had ever been mildly interested in to Daniel. Sadly, they had all fallen short. She would probably always love him. There was one thing she would not do, and that was marry a man who did not love her. It was different for a woman. Men did not need to be in love to give themselves to a person.

She would not be married because he felt guilty.

"Nothing has happened."

Even in the darkness of the folly she could see his eyebrow

rise. "Indeed? What would you say this was about?"

"We lost our heads."

"And you do this on a regular basis." He fairly growled the words.

"No. But, Daniel, can you tell me that you marry every woman you take liberties with?"

His frown turned blacker. She could tell he wanted to argue, but Lady Joanna saved her from any volley he would launch. The door squeaked open.

"Do hurry up. We do not have much time."

She smiled and turned to leave, but Daniel still held her hand. She looked back at him and shivered as he pulled her to him.

"I am not done with you."

In the next instant, he pulled her into his arms and gave her a quick, thoroughly mind-numbing kiss. She tasted the passion from before, his need, hers, and her body responded. She could not help it, would never be able to keep this reaction under control. Not now that he had touched her.

Before she was ready for it to end, it did. She swayed back to him, but Lady Joanna took matters into her own hands. She clamped a surprisingly strong hand down on her arm and jerked her away from Daniel.

By the time she pulled her out into the cool night air, some of Anna's sanity had returned. Unfortunately, so did some of her discomfiture.

"Please, do not harbor any thoughts that I have ever been interested in Daniel," Lady Joanna said.

She glanced at the older woman but said nothing. Anna could not make out her expression to see if she were trying to fool her. By the tone of her voice, Anna was sure she was deadly serious.

"There are things you do not know, things that I know he will not tell you. Not unless he is forced to."

Anna did not like it one bit. Here was a woman who claimed not to be his paramour, someone who should not know more than any distant aunt. But she knew intimate things about him. Things that one shared only with a lover or a spouse.

The lights of the house grew brighter the closer they got and Anna sighed with relief. She truly did not want to have any more awkward conversations. But even as she approached the lower terrace, Lady Joanna stayed her by touching her arm.

"Anna."

She forced herself to look at the woman and immediately wished she had not. The light was dim, but there was no hiding the amazing beauty of Lady Joanna. She stood several inches taller than Anna, curvy, and with the most amazing golden brown eyes. They drew everyone's attention.

"Daniel is obligated to do things, for the family. But know this, whatever he does is honorable."

"Of course."

"I have never been, and never will be, interested in Daniel that way. He is my nephew, more like a brother. He is not for me."

Anna studied the woman. Her expression was earnest, her tone serious.

"He is not for me either, Lady Joanna."

"Oh, Anna, he is for you. Both of you are just too dense to realize it." She sighed. "Let's get back. Your mother was extremely upset from what I understand."

"How did you know where to find me?"

Joanna smiled. Anna blinked. The older woman's face brightened, her eyes glowing, her pleasure easy for anyone to see. Her sharp features had softened. "I attended a few parties here myself before my husband died. I know the folly well."

Even as she smiled, sadness tinged her voice. This was not a woman looking for another lover, not yet at least. So many people thought Lady Joanna married her husband for money and status. No matter what the reasons, Anna could tell she missed her husband.

"Lady Joanna—"

"Considering the situation, please call me Jo."

Anna smiled. "Jo. I am in your debt for tonight."

They had reached the terrace and Anna heard a murmur as the guests started to spill out onto the terrace.

"No. I am in your debt. For the work we are in, Daniel takes himself a little too seriously. He needs someone to redirect his attention on...to lighten his load." She smiled as Anna opened her mouth to ask her just what she meant. "Brace yourself. Your mother is on her way."

Daniel slipped through French doors that, if he remembered correctly, led to the library...and a good amount of brandy.

He sighed with relief when he found it empty and located the brandy easy enough. He was pouring himself a glass when the door opened, light spilling into the room. Instantly, he was on guard, unable to see who the person was.

"Daniel?" Horace asked.

Daniel sighed and picked up the brandy. "Shut the door, Horace. I don't want to share this with anyone," he said, lifting the brandy glass.

Horace chuckled and did as Daniel asked. "I will only help you if you pour me a glass. I cannot take another glass of warm lemonade."

Daniel poured another glass. "Were you in search of

brandy?"

Horace took a drink and sighed. "No. I was sent to look for you."

Daniel frowned as he settled into a chair. "Who was looking for me?"

"Your mother. She was a bit upset when she could not find you."

"Ah, well, she has no reason to worry. Maybe I should go tell her I am okay."

Before he could rise, Horace waved him back in the chair. "I told her not to worry and she seemed to calm down after talking to Lady Joanna. Odd though, I have never seen her get so upset when you go missing."

"Joanna?" Daniel asked. "Why would she be upset?"

"No, your mother. She seemed beside herself when she could not find you. Odd reaction."

Of course she had. His mother had been on pins and needles since the Viper had returned. Understandable after the knifing incident. But he knew he would have to come up with something to explain his mother's reaction. Daniel knew that for all the years that his family had been friends with Horace, no one had told him of their work. Close friends were never to be told, not because they did not trust them. He had never told Sebastian, but he would trust his best friend with his life. But if they told friends, those friends could become targets for kidnapping. It was seen as something dishonorable to leave your friend open up to that.

"I think my mother wanted to find me off with a woman...as in to be found in an embarrassing situation."

Horace shook his head. "I don't follow."

"Mother wants me to marry. She was hoping if I got caught, I would do the honorable thing."

"Ah, and you would. You are so like your father in that

respect."

"Well, I guess it would not be a bad thing. I think I have come to a decision in that realm."

And just like that, he realized he had. When he had led Anna to the folly, he had known he would take her as a wife. One did not dally with a virgin, especially when she was your best friend's little sister. It was not a decision after the fact. He did not care if they had been caught because he had already made his decision before he touched her.

"Oh? And who would be the lucky girl? That Mortenson chit, the one with the merchant father?"

Daniel tried to remember what the woman looked like. He had a vague idea of a lot of teeth and a lot of brown hair, but that was all. Granted, he had danced a reel with her, but he could not conjure up her features. Of course, he could not. The only woman he had seen that night was Anna.

"No. If you can keep things quiet and promise not to tell my mother, I have decided on Lady Anna."

Horace frowned. "Really? I would think she was more of a bother than anything else."

Daniel blinked at Horace's harsh tone.

"I did not know you were well acquainted with Lady Anna."

Horace shook his head. "I am not, but I have seen her frequent areas she should not be. Women like that are a problem."

Daniel paused in taking another sip. "What do you mean?"

"Do-gooders are the worst of the lot. They never give you a moment's rest. Marry a chit like that and you will constantly be going to this fundraiser and that fundraiser. Before you know it, you haven't been to your club in six months or more."

Daniel laughed. "And you would know this being a bachelor?"

"I've seen my friends suffer through it."

"Hmm." As he turned the idea over in his mind, he realized that accompanying her would not be such a chore. While he wasn't happy about her traipsing back and forth by herself, Daniel did feel a certain sense of pride. Shallow women would have experienced what she did and not thought twice about it. Instead, Anna saw what she saw as faults to her character and changed them. In his opinion, the only thing she did was make herself more desirable.

"Mark my words, you marry that woman and you will lose all semblance of order in your life. They can't help but take over."

"She loves that orphanage, and I find it admirable that she took it on."

"And what of the area?"

"What of it? I know that Sebastian has people guard her constantly." He did not mention that he also had someone watching the orphanage. "What I want to know is why you would be in that part of town?"

"Uh...Well...a man has his needs."

Daniel laughed and waved away Horace's embarrassment. "I truly do not want to know anything about that."

"I should hope not," Horace grumbled into his glass before taking another long sip. Daniel looked out the French doors, his mind going back to the folly and Anna. He had told her that he would marry her. She had rebuffed him, but for once, he wanted it. He wanted to marry her. For the first time in all his years as an adult, thoughts of marriage, of loving the same woman every night, of watching her grow heavy with his child, did not send him into cold sweats. Instead, bone-deep need unfurled in him. This was not sexual need—although there was plenty of that entwined with a deeper feeling. Hope that he had not felt in years had heat rushing to his heart.

Good Lord, he wanted her. Not just tonight, and not in the lustful way he had when she had first gotten to London. He loved the way she laughed, the way she softened when she talked about her orphanage, and the way she said his name on a sigh when he leaned in to kiss her.

"Daniel?"

Horace's voice brought him back from his musings.

"I say, are you all right? You look like you've lost something."

Daniel shook his head. "No, actually gained something."

"Well, I hope this talk helped you." Horace looked hopeful, as if he would be saving Daniel from a fate worse than death. He could set his old family friend right, but why bother him.

"You have helped me immensely."

"Dinner will be starting soon. We best be getting back."

"You go ahead. I will be there in a moment."

Horace nodded and slowly walked to the door. Once he was alone, Daniel thought about the ramifications of his feelings. He had not planned on marrying, and part of him still believed that to be the best way to go. But he knew that in the back of his mind, he had been waiting. Waiting for Anna.

But he was in no position truly. He needed to solve the riddle of the Viper, lest he put her in harm's way. It was bad enough that she had been seen, that men were now following her. He would not put her in more danger by marrying her.

That made him all the more determined to find the Viper and be done with it.

"You say they disappeared together?" the man known as Viper said.

The stupid footman nodded.

"What else?"

144

"I do know that Lady Anna returned with Lady Joanna."

That brought his head around, his sharp gaze studying the footman. "She returned with Lady Joanna? Are you sure?"

"Yes, sir." The weasel squeaked out the answer.

"Are you telling me the woman most think Bridgerton to be courting returned with his paramour?"

He nodded again.

He threw the footman some coins and moved toward the windows of his room. "Leave, and if I hear you tell anyone my name, your death will not only happen, it will be slow and painful."

There was another squeak, the sound of shuffling feet, and then the door closed behind him. He truly did not know if what he heard was correct, but it sounded about right. Bridgerton had been sniffing around Lady Anna for some days now, and it was apparent he wanted her. But what was Joanna doing? And what little self-respect did Lady Anna have that she would allow Bridgerton's whore to accompany her back, giving her an alibi? That just did not sound correct. Lady Anna had quite a bit of pride.

"Jenkins?"

His valet came into the room.

"Yes, sir?"

"I need you to find out what is going on between Lady Joanna and Bridgerton."

"I do not need to find out. I know."

He glanced at him. "And?"

"Nothing. They act more like brother and sister at times."

"Indeed."

"And I do know a lot of those old family retainers are still around. All those old spies who worked for Harold."

That gave him pause. "Is there a chance she knew of her

husband's activities?"

"Not sure about that, sir. The theory was that he married her to have a pretty woman on his arm."

He sneered. "He was vain enough for that. I wondered how long it would take my supervisor to kill him."

"Sir?"

"Nothing. Check and see what is going on with Lady Anna and Lady Joanna. To corner Bridgerton, I need to know which of them means more to him."

But he was pretty sure he knew which one it was...and it would be his pleasure to kill the little bitch in front of the bastard.

Chapter Thirteen

Daniel took a gelding out for a hard ride the next morning. Early. He'd had no sleep thanks to the encounter with Anna. She had been relieved, but he was suffering still. What little time he had slept he had been in the midst of torture. It was all a haze of Anna naked in his arms, in his bed, her long limbs wrapped around him, her breathless sigh echoing in his ears. Then he watched in horror as a faceless man appeared, wrapping his hands around her arms to pull her away from him. No matter how hard he tried to follow, he seemed stuck in that bed, his body unable to move.

The impotent feeling was something akin to what he'd felt the night before. He had watched from the sidelines as Joanna stayed by Anna's side, making sure everyone knew it had been them together and not Daniel and Anna. Dammit, he should be happy. He had decided to marry her, but she had told him there was no reason to worry. That marriage would not be needed. He had never thought to marry, especially to a woman who turned him inside out. But there was something in the way she reacted to his suggestion that cut him deep. He was missing something. He knew that without a doubt, but he could not figure out what it was. And he knew that this growing entanglement was going to get worse before it was over. Somehow though, he felt helpless to stop it.

Shaking his head, he reigned in his mount and turned to

go back to the house. He heard the crack a second before his horse reared. He held on, barely. Knowing what he had heard was a shot, he calmed his horse down as much as possible, then goaded him on. Another shot hit a tree behind him, but he did not stop. He had no weapon with him and he was a sitting target if he didn't get back to the house. Within moments, the house came into view, but he did not slow. He galloped right into the stable area before he slowed down. Both he and gelding were out of breath by the time they arrived. He said nothing to anyone as he returned the horse to the stable.

He did not slow down to talk to anyone until he got to his room. He sent for Jack immediately.

"What is going on, my lord?"

"I think someone just took a shot at me."

Jack's busy grey eyebrows rose. "Are you sure?"

He told Jack what happened.

"Aye, that is troubling. Are you going to tell Lady Adelaide?"

"No. She is beside herself in worry about the Viper. If she hears this, she is likely to order me home. I cannot leave Anna here unprotected."

"Aye. I think we could get Lord Simon down here for that."

"I thought he was attending things on his estate."

"Aye, but Jo has been in contact with him. He could come down in no time at all."

It would be smart. His cousin Simon was young, but well trained. And he would guard Anna with his life—that much Daniel was certain of. But the truth of the matter was Daniel could not allow that. He rebelled against the idea of any eligible man to attend to Anna's safety.

"No."

Jack studied him for a moment then relented.

"Go to Jo and get her to meet me in the library. I think it

should be clear this time of the morning. I need to talk to her."

Anna found herself in the library again, this time trying to find something to read. She'd had little to no sleep the night before, the problems of Daniel turning over in her head. She hoped she'd dissuaded him from talking to her mother, but she was not so sure. She knew exactly how her mother would react if Daniel proposed marriage. She closed her eyes for a moment. God, her one dream and nightmare combined in one irritating man. How could she want him so badly, need to feel his touch more so now than before last night?

Her mother had said nothing to her this morning, so she assumed that Daniel had not talked to her. She had yet to see the man in question this morning and she wanted to make sure that he understood her position. She found a few books and set them on the desk in front of the massive window that looked out onto the front drive. She accidentally hit the bottom book. The tomes toppled to the ground. Anna rolled her eyes and knelt to pick them up. She could not seem to do anything right. Before she could rise, the door opened and she heard footsteps, then Daniel's voice.

"I told Jack to be quick about it, but I did not expect him to get you down here so quickly."

Joanna laughed. "I am an early riser. It is that or I don't get breakfast in my house."

"Indeed."

"Now what was so important that you talk to me right now?" Joanna asked.

The doors shut. "Someone took a shot at me this morning."

"Good Lord, Daniel, you have to take this business seriously."

"There is not much I can do." She could hear the shrug in his voice. As if it was no problem that someone had shot at him.

"If you do not start a real investigation into this Viper, I will tell your mother. The War Department might not care about what you do, but your mother will."

"Give it a rest, Jo. I can take care of myself."

"You sound a bit too much like your uncle." The worry in Jo's voice caused Anna to start worrying herself. She had known Daniel's uncle died several months earlier, and Joanna was under suspicion by most of the ton for poisoning him.

"Let it go. I have inquiries out and I will use more precautions from now on."

"And Lady Anna? Do you realize that she is now in the sights of the Viper? What will you do about her?"

She had heard enough. She rose to her feet and asked, "Yes, what about Lady Anna?"

Chapter Fourteen

Daniel watched in horror as Anna crossed her arms beneath her breasts and glared at him. Every nightmare he had ever imagined had not come close to the one he was living at the moment. In his entire life, he had never made so many mistakes...and definitely not since he'd taken his father's place. How could he have stepped into the library and started discussing something like this without checking to see if they were alone? He knew why, and she was shooting daggers with her eyes at him right now. Dressed in a light green sprigged dress, with the sunlight shining behind her, she looked like a very grumpy avenging angel.

He could hear the ticking of the clock, the occasional burst of conversation from the other attendees, the beating of his heart.

"Are neither of you going to explain?"

He could feel Jo staring at him, urging him to explain. After last night, it was his place, but he really did not know what to say. All of his worst fears were staring at him right now.

"I think you misunderstood what we were talking about," Jo offered.

"Indeed."

Her tone told Daniel she would not believe anything either of them would make up. Her brilliant blue eyes studied him with defiance a lesser man would cower from.

"Fine. I...I am a spy."

She said nothing, her expression now unreadable.

"The night that you happened upon me—"

"When you were stabbed?"

"Yes."

He said nothing else, so she said, "Go on."

"I was attacked that night. You were seen by the hired assassin."

Her face paled at the word assassin, but he could not sugarcoat it for her. She wanted the truth, she would have it.

"And now I am in the sights of this Viper person?"

"It seems that you foiled his plans. Which irritates him."

"Hmm."

She turned to look out at the front drive, but he could feel her moving away from him completely. He'd expected this, but to experience it was another thing. Most of the ton felt he was no better than a Frenchman. Even if what he did saved countless lives, that the Bridgertons had been doing this for centuries, most of his friends would give him the cut direct if they knew what he did.

"He has sent inquires around the area."

She glanced around, alarm clearly written on her face. "The orphanage?"

"No, they are fine. Everything this man does is personal."

"But if anything happened to the orphanage..." She swallowed and closed her eyes. "I just could not bear it."

Joanna glanced at him, but he said nothing. With a sigh, the older woman said, "You need not worry. Daniel has made sure it is well protected."

Anna nodded, then turned away again.

"You think there might have been a problem here. You were shot at?"

"It was nothing—"

"Tell me everything."

Her voice told him she would accept nothing less than the entire story. He exchanged a glance with Jo, who shrugged.

"I was out riding."

"You did not get hurt?" Her voice held not emotion.

"No."

"When did you hear about the Viper person asking about me?"

He hesitated, then said, "Two days after the attack."

A beat of silence filled the room. "I see."

It was then that he realized the timing would look suspicious to her. He wanted to deny it, but would she believe him? When she turned around, her face still held no expression, her eyes colder than the north wind. Of course, she would not. The level of deception was enough to make any good woman ready to kill.

"Are you going to tell anyone?"

She frowned. "No. Telling someone would expose you. Why on earth would I do that?"

She said it with such disbelief that he had to fight the need to laugh, but he knew she would take it the wrong way.

"I understand you might be upset."

"Upset? Upset is too minimal of a word to describe what I feel at the moment."

He stepped toward her but she held up her hand to stop him. The gesture stabbed at his heart. She could not bear to even look at him.

"Don't. I need time to think about this."

He wanted to demand an answer, beg her forgiveness. It was too soon for that. "Of course."

He continued to stare at her, not knowing what else to say.

Jo cleared her throat. "Daniel, why don't you talk to Jack? You need to send a note to Simon to let him know what is going on."

He didn't want to leave, but Jo had left him with no choice. Granted, leaving was probably a better idea than standing there staring at her like a simpleton.

"Anna..."

"I said I needed time to think about it. Please at least give me that courtesy."

He nodded once and then left the room. The moment he stepped outside the library, Jack appeared by his right elbow.

"All well, my lord?"

"Yes." He sighed. "I mean no. We have been found out by Lady Anna."

When the old retainer said nothing, he looked at him. The smile he offered puzzled Daniel.

"What are you grinning at?"

"I told you that she was a sharp one."

"Indeed. My worry is now if she will reveal us."

"Oh, no worries in that quarter, my lord. She's a good one. She will keep all your secrets."

"Hmm, well I cannot worry about that right now. I need you to contact Lord Simon. Let him know what happened today. But make sure he knows that we do not need him here yet. I just want him to know what has been happening."

"Yes, sir."

Without any other comments, Jack left him. Daniel needed to get out, do some riding, but he knew that was out of the question now. One of the people attending the house party was a killer. Probably not the Viper, but someone he'd sent. Which would be easy to do. When the bastard had targeted Daniel's father, he'd had many destitute aristocracy help him in his quest. It wasn't that hard to find someone who had moneylenders knocking at their door.

He climbed the steps trying to think of everyone in attendance. He could get the list from Greenwood, but that would definitely draw attention to them. And who was to say that the older or younger Greenwood wasn't the one who was indebted to the Viper.

He was more worried about Anna. The question was whether she would forgive him or not? He remembered the pain in her eyes, the coldness of her voice... If she did forgive him, it would not be any time soon.

Anna said nothing for a few minutes. Truly, she could not think of anything to say. She was still trying to comprehend everything that had just come to light.

"Will you truly not tell anyone?"

Jo's voice held a hint of worry. Anna could understand, but it did not mean she was happy about it.

"You do not know me well, so I will allow for that. I will never tell anyone what any of you do. I am presuming you are one of them?"

She nodded.

"I would never put any of you, especially Daniel, in harm's way."

"Thank you."

She turned around and looked out at the drive once again. It seemed so pleasant, such a brilliant, beautiful day. But at the moment, she felt cold. She could not seem to warm herself. As the silence stretched, she could feel the tension rise. It was not coming from her. She was frozen. But rather the fear was pouring off Lady Joanna in waves.

"I gave you my word. I will not expose you."

"I believe you."

Anna turned and looked at the older woman. What would make a woman such as her become entangled in such a mess?

"I married into it."

Anna flushed and looked away. Lady Joanna laughed but there was little joy in it.

"No. I do not mind."

Anna looked back to her again. "I just do not understand. Why would you put yourself in jeopardy? You could marry again, have children."

The smile she offered seemed a little sad. "No. That is not for me. I...tried for years with my late husband. It was not to be."

"You know, according to my sister-in-law, it is sometimes the man's fault."

"I dare say most problems that arise are men's fault. But in this case it is not. Harold had children with his first and second wives. We were not so lucky."

"So now you do this."

"It is what my husband trained me for."

Anna felt her eyes widen at the statement. "Your husband made you a spy?"

"My husband was a spy. As was Daniel's father. But...I believe that is something you need to discuss with Daniel."

"So, there isn't any..."

"Any?" It took a moment, but Joanna's expression cleared. "Oh. No. There is nothing going on between Daniel and me, just as I told you last night. There has never been anyone but my husband for me."

A small sharp jab of envy bit into Anna's heart at the wealth of love she heard in the other woman's voice. She had known those relationships existed. She watched her brother and cousin fall in love, marry for it. But it was not for her. The one man she had always loved had just informed her that he had been paying attention to her because she was in danger. That did not speak of undying love or devotion...at least not to her.

Joanna chuckled. "Oh, Daniel is in for a very hard time with you, my lady."

Anna focused on her for a moment, then looked away. "I said I would not cause you any problems and I mean it. I might not always seem like the brightest one of the bunch, but I am not stupid."

The older woman cocked her head to one side as she studied her. "I believe that you are far more intelligent than you let on to be."

Anna opened her mouth to refute it.

"Do not lie to me and insult my intelligence. I am not saying it is a bad thing. But I believe that even Daniel, a man who rarely underestimates anyone, man or woman, might have done so with you."

"That isn't that important."

Lady Joanna said nothing, her expression letting Anna know exactly how she felt.

"Yes. Well." She ran her hands down the front of her dress. "I guess I need to retire, or something. Or...I don't know."

"Act as you normally do. Do not deviate from your normal routines. Just act like everything is normal."

Anna nodded. "I wish it was."

"Sometimes not getting what we wished for is a blessing in disguise."

Anna had nothing to say to that but nod. As she slipped out the door and walked to her room, her mind bubbled with the ramifications of what had just transpired. Daniel was a spy, and not only that, apparently a very powerful one...trained by his father. She barely noticed the people she passed, mostly house staff. Once she reached her room, she shut the door and leaned back against it.

A strange sense of calmness slipped over her. It was decidedly odd that at the moment she had no feelings...she was numb. What had she been thinking? Daniel would never be interested in a woman like her. No good men could. She had proven that with Dewhurst.

She walked to her bed as the memories from three years ago blew to the forefront of her brain. There had been many suitors before him. With her dowry and connections, she was a catch. Oh, she was attractive enough, but she knew those two things sealed the deal, so to speak.

She threw herself on the bed and rolled over onto her back. She closed her eyes and allowed the events of those last few weeks before her cousin's abduction flitted through her mind. She had been so stupid, so naive. Was it any wonder that Dewhurst had used her so easily? She had been like a lamb to the slaughter.

He had known how badly she needed the attention. He had found her weakness and played with her. Daniel's escapades had been getting out of control, and having a man who seemingly did not need her fortune, had his choice of women, focus his attention on her... She had fallen for it, ready to throw caution to the wind. If Dewhurst had asked her to run off to Gretna Greene, she would have gone. That carefree feeling had dissolved the moment she found out about his duplicity. She had been duped, used, and very nearly lost her good name. It was something she would not do again. She did not know how to react to this latest development. Daniel had always been a friend, someone to look up to. Someone she loved. She had realized last night that she was still in love with him. It was no longer just a girlhood crush.

What would she do? She did not know. She would never

expose him, put him in danger. But other than that...

With a sigh, she picked herself up and decided to get out. She needed time to think and clean, fresh country air always seemed to help with that. After what had happened to Daniel she knew she would have to stay close to the house, but she needed solitude. As she pulled the bell cord, she prayed that it would help this time.

Daniel eased his way through the music room as he tried to ignore the bellowing of one of Lord Tate's girls. Everyone faced forward, seemingly interested in the untalented chit. Bloody hell, the girl could not sing. In fact, there was a good chance she was strangling a cat.

He skimmed the room for Anna and suppressed a sigh. It seemed that he spent most of his time looking for her these days. She was beginning to become an obsession of his, one that he did not know if he would ever be able to control. She had become his first thought in the morning, his last thought at night, and the woman who refused to let him sleep as she invaded his dreams.

When he could not find her, he located her mother, sitting next to his. Damn. He had to look inconspicuous moving to the other side of the room, but at least it would appear he was approaching his mother.

"Daniel."

He leaned down to allow his mother to kiss his cheek.

"Mother. Lady Victoria."

Anna's mother bowed her head.

"I thought you would be out riding, or doing something manly." His mother could always make him feel as if he were a lad in leading strings.

A twinge of guilt stabbed his stomach. He had not told his mother of the earlier altercation. Furthermore, he had ordered both Jo and Jack to secrecy. He pushed the feelings aside, knowing that alerting his mother would only make his investigation impossible.

"I went out for a ride this morning and was not in the mood for the hunt they had planned this afternoon." He glanced around the room. "I take it Lady Anna decided not to attend the music this afternoon?"

Lady Victoria made a face. "No. Anna likes music, but she said she was not in the mood. She took a book outside to read."

Alarm shifted through him. "Alone?"

The tone of his voice caused Lady Victoria to look at him curiously. "Well, I believe she was going to find a nice bench in the garden and read. She tends to spend a lot of time outdoors when we are in the country. She misses the freedom when we are in town. It is actually warm for this time of year."

He glanced at his mother and noticed her almost imperceptible nod. She was worried also.

"Well, ladies, I think I shall take a stroll outside."

With little ceremony, he slipped out the French doors and into the garden. When he could not find Anna in the gardens near the house, his worry turned into panic. Then he saw her sitting close to the front lawn, the book she had brought to read sitting beside her on the bench. He could not see her since her back was to him. As he approached, he took the time to drink in the sight of her.

His need for her had been growing for years. Now he could not seem to control it. Their interactions did little to control his appetite. In truth, he was now ravenous for her. For a man who was used to control, he did not like it. Anything—drink, gambling, women—that made you lose your control was bad for a man. His father had taught him that. It had been one of his earliest lessons.

But now, with the afternoon sun picking up the gold curls

peeking out from under her hat, he did not think of that. All he did think of was pulling that hat off her head and watching as those curls fell about her shoulders.

He approached silently, thinking she would not hear his approach. But before he could reach her, she glanced over her shoulder at him, as if she knew he was there.

"I thought you would be out on the hunt."

There was no condemnation in her voice, or in her expression. It was then that he realized he had expected it.

"After my morning I thought it best to stay close to the house."

She frowned. "Whatever do you mean?"

Inwardly, he cursed. Lying to Anna was difficult, and he knew at the moment no matter what story he improvised, she would know it. Worse, he didn't want to lie to her.

He took the last few steps and sat beside her on the bench. "As I said, someone took a shot at me this morning."

"Of course. You told me to stay close to the house." She turned around and looked over her shoulder at the house. "As you can see, I am very close."

"I also did not want to leave you alone."

Her brow puckered in a frown. "Why ever not?"

"I told you that someone is after you."

She sighed and looked out over the winter lawn. "Yes, so you and Jo say. I doubt there is much to worry about though. What use would harming me do this Viper person?"

Because it would destroy me. So spoke his heart, but he could not bring himself to say the words aloud. He did not think she would believe him if he did tell her. At the moment, he knew she thought he had seduced her so that he could stay close to her. She would never believe he had done it because he had to stay close to her. Being in close contact with Anna crumbled any will he had to behave as he should.

"He has little logic. You have thwarted his plans and I am sure he is irritated. He would think it imperative to pay you back."

She nodded, but said nothing. The silence stretched.

"Anna." She did not look at him. "Look at me."

She did then, her expression calm.

"I know I do not have the right to ask, but you will keep this all a secret, yes?"

Something that looked close to disappointment moved over her face before it disappeared. "I gave you my word."

Then she turned from him. He wanted to grab her, shake her, get some kind of reaction. But at the moment, if he touched her Daniel wasn't too sure he could control himself.

"I want you to be very careful. Being out here by yourself is not a good idea."

"There are plenty of people around."

He nodded in agreement. "But I would rather you stay in groups."

Another sigh. "Of course."

"And it would be better if you actually pretend to be in search of a husband."

With precise movements, she turned to him then. "Indeed? And how would I go about doing that?"

"Stop avoiding the activities. Dance at night. Spend time with eligible bachelors."

She said nothing in response, her gaze studying him. When she finally answered, he was fighting the urge to fidget like a young boy. "As you wish."

She rose, and the sense of losing her washed over him. This was not the Anna he knew. Even in her more reserved moments the last few years, she was not this...composed. She had taken her passion for life and delved into the foundling home. He grabbed at her hand as if he needed a lifeline. She stilled but did not look at him.

"Anna?"

"I said I would do as you ask, which means I should return now."

He nodded and willed himself to release her hand.

"Good day, my lord."

She said nothing more as she walked toward the house. Her easy grace pulled the attention of several of the men in the area. They watched her, the same lustful longing in their expression that he felt in his gut. But there was something more from him, and he knew it. It scared the bloody hell out of him, but at that moment he did not think there was a way to stop this.

He had spent the last few years denying he was in love with the one woman he could never had. Now he had to do everything to keep her safe, or die trying.

Anna sighed as she approached her door later that night. She had done what Daniel had asked. Of course, she would. Even knowing his interest in her was purely for her safety, even though he had broken her heart, she would do as he asked. She was powerless not to. She knew he had asked it for her safety. Knowing that his life was at stake made her compliance critical.

She slipped through her door, wanting nothing but to dissolve into dreams. It had been a long day, one that she would care not to think about. She had told Gerty to go to bed. The poor woman had been up at the crack of dawn helping Anna, and she had not had the heart to expect Gerty to wait up for her. Of course, now Anna had to try and get out of her dress by herself.

She closed the door behind her and set her dance card on

the dressing table to the right of the door.

"I see that you were smart enough to return to your room by yourself." She gasped and turned to find an enraged Daniel bearing down on her. "I do not want to think what would happen if you had not."

Chapter Fifteen

Anna's heart slammed against her chest as she tried to calm herself. She squinted but could only make the outline of Daniel's body near the window.

"What in heavens are you thinking? Why are you here?"

He moved out of the shadows, dressed in the same clothes he had worn downstairs. He had done his best to appear to ignore her, and she had held her end of the bargain also. But it had been harder than ever. Even as she had told herself to ignore him, she would watch him out of the corner of her eye.

"I could ask you the same thing."

Every word was punctuated with anger. When she looked up, irritation defined the lines of his face.

"I have no idea what you are talking about. But I do not appreciate you popping into my room this way."

She tried to move around him, but he stalked toward her. She didn't realize she had retreated back until she felt the wall at her back.

"You do not appreciate it? Do you know what I do not appreciate, Anna?"

She could not speak. Fury cascaded off him in waves. Rage burned in his eyes. In her life, she had never seen Daniel so mad. She shook her head.

"No? Let me enlighten you. Seeing a woman who allowed

me certain liberties just last night allowing men to slobber on her all night is enough to make any man irritated."

There was a feral look clouding his golden brown eyes. She could not seem to look away. Shadows danced over his face, thrown there by the candle light, making him seem more ominous. Her blood pounded in her veins, her head started to spin.

"Y-you told me to do it. You said to act like I was looking for a husband."

He placed a hand on either side of her head, effectively caging her in. "Yes. A husband. Not a protector."

The implication of his words sent the rage he had been displaying sizzling through her, bursting up through the fear she had felt. She placed her hands on her chest and shoved him. The incredulous look on his face would have made her laugh, if she could find any kind of humor. But at the moment, anger and pain surged through her.

"How dare you? I did exactly as you asked. I played the part."

He looked at her. "Indeed? I do not believe I told you to dress like a tart."

Mortification sent a wave of heat to her face. She had picked the dress on purpose. It was one Colleen had convinced her to buy. Bright red, cut to reveal just enough of her bosom. She had always felt beautiful in it. But now she felt tawdry.

"I do not look like a tart. In fact, I am wearing much more material than that widow you were paying attention to."

The moment she said the words, she wanted to bite her tongue. He tried to pounce on her mistake.

"A widow?"

She crossed her arms beneath her breasts. "Lady Waldrip."

The anger ebbed from his features. "I did not think you noticed what I was doing. She was just a means to an end."

She couldn't look him in the face. "Believe me, I did not. It was noticed by several people."

"Who then had to say something to you?"

She nodded.

"I apologize. I thought it best that people thought my attention were elsewhere."

"That is not my point. My point is my dress is no less respectable than hers."

The moment she said it, his features tightened again and she realized her mistake. "Yes, let's talk about this dress. Does your brother know you bought such a dress?"

She did not like the lethal tone his voice had just taken. She was downright sick of hearing him complain about her choice in dresses. It was not as if she asked for the role she had been thrown into.

"I answer to no man."

Everything about him seemed to still. "What did you just say?"

Air clogged up in her throat as her heart beat slammed against her chest again. "I said I answer to no man."

She could barely hear the words, even though she hoped she had made her point. His nostrils flared, his eyes narrowed. He caged her in with his arms again, but this time, he leaned into her. The heat of his body warmed hers. His scent surrounded her.

"Are you challenging me, Anna?"

She opened her mouth but no words came out. There was a darkness about him, something lethal that she had never seen before. She should be scared out of her mind—and she was, to a point. There was another emotion that took over. Desire. Passion. *Need.*

"I don't think it very wise to challenge me. I had a rough

night."

She swallowed at the way he looked at her, as if he was here to claim her. Even as her mind told her body not to respond, she did just that. Her breasts grew heavy, achy for his touch. Her skin prickled with anticipation.

"Y-you? I had to deal with fortune hunters all night."

He leaned in and nuzzled her neck. His breath feathered over her skin before she felt him nip at her neck. "I had to watch while you danced with them, letting them paw all over you."

"I did not."

"I do not know when it became such a trial; watching men touch you, act as if they had a chance with you."

"You..." She swallowed again, her throat suddenly dry. "I thought I was supposed to do that."

He nodded. "But I did not think of how it would feel."

He had laid not a hand on her, only the touch of his lips over her sensitive flesh. But she felt trapped...captured...entranced.

"How did it make you feel?"

He sighed, sending another gust of breath over her skin.

"Daniel?"

"It made me want to do murder." He snarled the words and something deep and dark inside of her started to unfurl and blossom. It raced through her body, sending out ribbons of heat lancing through her veins.

She turned her head and kissed his temple.

"Danny," she whispered.

For a moment, he stilled. The air between them grew heated as he turned to look at her. Her heart turned over the moment she saw his eyes. Her own desire was there, reflected back to her in the depths of his golden gaze. With a groan, he

168

collapsed against her and then pulled her away from the wall. As if he were starved, he took her mouth, feasting on her. This was no tender kiss of a lover, but one of a man pushed to the brink. Heat flared, spiraled through her as he pulled her to the bed. He quickly turned them around so that the back of her legs were against the mattress. He stood there, slanting his mouth over hers, deepening the kiss, completely and absolutely destroying her.

She wanted to tear herself away, wanted to stop the complete attack on her senses. It was as if she had no control over her body.

He pulled away, cupping her face. "Stop me now. Don't let me do this if you do not want it. This is your last chance."

Every word was ragged with need for her. For her. She had never had a man want her this way, just her, Anna. The fear dissolved. What he felt was there on his face, in his gaze. He didn't care if she had a large dowry or if her brother was a powerful earl. She did not even think this had anything to do with protecting her. This was for her. In this one moment, all he wanted was Anna, and it was enough to brush away her other worries.

Without breaking eye contact, she drew in a deep breath and raised her hands, wrapping them around his wrists. Everything she had ever wanted was here, right before her, in his eyes.

"Take me, Danny."

Every barrier Daniel had erected tumbled down, demolished by the need he heard in her voice. With a groan, he tumbled them over onto the bed, her body soft and willing beneath his. Never in his life had his desire for a woman burned him up so, but this woman, this time, was different.

He devoured her then, taking her lips in a bruising, almost

painful kiss. Instead of shying away, Anna dove into the kiss with him, her tongue dancing along his as he thrust it between her lips. As before, the taste of her burst through him, sending another wave of heat shooting through his blood.

Gone was the calculated lover who could talk any woman into bed, thrill her with a well-planned seduction. He slanted his mouth over hers, reveling in her response. Lord, she was amazing. But it was not enough. He needed more. He needed to feel her flesh against his.

He pulled back enough to claw at her bodice. The flimsy material slipped down, her breasts spilling out.

"Danny." He could hear the embarrassment in her voice but he paid no heed. In the folly the night before, it had been dark and he could not see anything. Even what he glimpsed in the carriage had not prepared him for the sight now before him. In the dim flickering light of candles, he could see the beauty that was Anna.

She had always been petite, but not too thin. Her breasts were not plentiful, but perfectly shaped, tipped with the most amazing rosebud nipples. With a shaking hand, he slipped his fingers up and over one nipple, loving the way it responded. He knew touching would not be enough. He bent his head and took the nipple into his mouth. Oh God, it was better than the night before. He could feel her heart racing as he slipped his other hand to her breast to tease it while he feasted. She speared her hands through his hair, her fingers molding to the back of his head. With every little gasp and moan she was driving him crazy. She shifted beneath him, rubbed against him, begged him. It was the most precious sound he had ever heard.

There was no doubt in his mind that he wanted her, needed her in a way that he had never needed a woman. It was the reason he had tried to stay away, but there was no turning back now. Even as his mind told him it was wrong, his body knew perfection...and that was Anna.

It did not take him long to get the rest of her clothes off. He tossed the gown behind him and looked down at the woman he had been in love with most of his adult life. Lord, she was a sight to see. Her alabaster skin glowed in the candlelight, her lips were rosy from his kisses, her hair a tangle of curls strewn across the bed.

"Danny? What?"

He looked at her, really looked at her, and realized she was embarrassed. Of course she was. No matter what went on the night before, she was still a virgin.

"Nothing. I...Lord, you are beautiful."

She blushed, and he found the sight arresting. He wasn't one for maidenly gestures, but he knew this was genuine.

"You do not have to say these things. The fact that you want me is enough."

He had said so many things to women, called them beautiful and meant it at the time. But his tongue refused to cooperate with him now. He needed to explain to her so much...but found himself unable to say the words. In his heart, he knew he loved her, had for years. But that would not soothe her now, and she would not believe anything he said. The only thing for him to do was to show her.

"Anna," he said, but he knew his voice must have sounded odd to her. It did to him. She must have thought he was having second thoughts because she sat up and grabbed the front of his shirt.

The ripping of the fabric was the most erotic sound he had heard. Her hand went to his breeches, fumbled against his as he tried to undo the buttons.

She laughed, the sound of it low, sexy, happy. A fire shot straight to his cock.

When his manhood sprang free, she did not act the gentle virgin that he knew she was. Instead, she wrapped her hand around it, her fingers slipping over his sensitive flesh. Lord, she was a good study, and dangerous. Very dangerous. She leaned forward and all he could see was her golden head, that erotic mouth edging closer to his cock. He knew now he could not wait, he could not go slowly like he had the night before. And even if he wanted to, his Anna was not going to allow it to happen. He could not allow her to pleasure him in such a way, it just would not work. He would lose himself the moment he slipped between those pink lips.

With a harsh groan, he pulled her back and followed her down on the bed again. With little finesse, he stationed his member at her entrance and entered her.

He watched her face, waited for her to tell him to stop. Daniel should have known better. Her eyes closed, her mouth curved into a secret smile and she arched back, exposing her throat.

"Anna."

Her eyes fluttered then slowly opened.

He had been frustrated these past few years by the fact she had hidden her feelings from him. Now though, everything she felt showed in her gaze. Passion deepened the blue color, and something else, something primal. She wanted him on a level that he knew she did not understand even if he did. Seeing it there sent a shot of lust roaring through him, and he pulled back then pushed through her maiden head.

The tiny gasp told him he had hurt her and he leaned down, setting his forehead against hers.

"Anna, I am sorry I hurt you."

He waited for tears, waited for her to tell him to stop. But he should have known better. His Anna would never act like a virginal miss would be expected to.

The smile she gave him was filled with satisfaction and tenderness.

"No worries, Danny."

Testing, he pulled out and then slowly slipped back into her tight sheath. Her muscles clung to him as he pushed all the way back in. In response, her eyes closed as she moaned, a sound that vibrated out of her throat. She arched against him again, her body fluid beneath him, moving with him. He bent his head and took a perfect rosy nipple into his mouth as she moaned his name, her pleasure washing over him, sending need racing over his nerve endings. Everything he wanted to say, everything he wanted to show her slipped away. Blatant primal need replaced it. With everything he had, he tried to hold back, but she planted her feet on the bed and pushed against him, her passage clinging to him. The moment before he lost it, he reached down and pressed against the tiny bundle of nerves.

"Danny!"

She came apart beneath him, her body convulsing, her muscles pulling his cock further inside of her. He could not keep himself in check any longer. Before he could even think, his release was upon him. He shouted her name, the pain of holding back from her all these years exploded as he lost himself. He poured his seed into her, his orgasm seemingly going on forever.

Long moments later, he dropped beside her on the bed, his body slick with exertion. Without hesitation, she moved to him, curling against him, her hand slipping over his chest and resting on his heart.

Again he found himself unable to say anything, unable to tell her exactly what was in his heart. Damn, the woman had him in tangles. What was new about that? Nothing. From the moment she had arrived in London looking for a husband at the fresh age of ten and eight, she had held him captive. And now she had truly ensnared him. They needed to make plans...and quickly. While he had not wanted to do it this way, he did not think they had any time to waste. She needed the protection of his name...and fast. Sebastian would not be happy about it, but there could be no helping it. He had not done the honorable thing and stayed away. Hell, he had not even taken precautions. There could even be a babe growing in her belly right now. No, there was no time to waste.

"Anna?"

Her even breathing told him that she had fallen asleep. He wanted to wake her up and demand her acceptance of his suit. But he knew that she was tired. She had not slept well the night before, and today had been a trying day for both of them. The moment she woke up, he would definitely get her acceptance.

It was the last thought he had before he drifted off to sleep.

Chapter Sixteen

Anna came awake with a start, terror pounding in her veins, screaming in her head. She had been having the most disturbing dream that involved dark alleys and Daniel bleeding. Her heart beat against her chest, her body shivering with the fear she felt for him. With a sigh, she lay back down and came up hard against a very solid male form. Panic surged, her terror of the dream melting into the present, but it only took her a moment to remember she did not sleep alone by choice.

Daniel.

She rose again and looked at him. Even in sleep he looked a bit dangerous...or was that her perception of him now. She had always seen him as the playmate, the easygoing one. But this was not the man she knew. There was something so dangerous about him, something that frightened her. Deep down though, there was something else, something that corresponded to this side of him. This man took what he wanted, damned the consequences. Anna had to admit that she loved him as much as the Daniel she had known before.

Loved.

God, she did still love him. Or maybe she was just falling in love with him. How could she have been in love with a man she apparently did not know that well? But this Daniel—Danny—he was someone she could love. She knew she still didn't know all of him. There was a bit of him he still kept hidden from her, but she could wait. And while she did, she could definitely make use of the body in front of her.

He had always been fit, but she did not know exactly how beautiful he would be. He turned to his side and she sighed. Sinewy muscles bunched as he reached for her. He slipped his arm around her waist and pulled her against him. It was then she felt the flesh against her, and even after everything, she could feel herself blush.

"What are you thinking about?"

His chest vibrated against her back and she shivered.

"I was thinking I did not know just how pretty you would be without any clothes."

He chuckled as those talented hands moved over her stomach then up to her breasts. He caressed the underside of her breast then moved to her nipple. Heat built, liquid poured through her veins. She couldn't think when he did that, when he touched her like this.

"I have never been called pretty before."

"What?"

Her brain was a blank slate against the pleasure he was giving her. His hand slid down her body, his fingers slipping inside her. She was already damp, needy.

"Danny."

As if he could no longer hold back, he pulled up and rolled her over onto her back. He covered her body with his as he balanced his weight on his hands. She looked up to the man who had just taken her on a journey she would never forget, her body already humming for the next trip. His hair was a mess, his sleepy eyes dark with need, and she wanted him. There was no way around it, she had to have him, needed him in a way that she surely would end up regretting. But at the moment, she didn't care. Her heart was stuttering, her breasts ached, her body yearned. How could this be possible? All he had to do was touch her and she lost all thought. It was not something she was happy about. She did not lose control, not to anyone.

"Anna."

She was not sure if she heard her name, but she saw his lips move. The serious expression on his face scared her. Oh God, she did not think she would be able to let him go, but she knew she would have to. He did not love her and she refused to marry without love. She reached up and cupped his cheek.

"Please, Danny."

Without closing his eyes, he lowered his head and kissed her gently. This was not the demanding, consuming kiss from earlier. This was soft as a rose petal, but something else was there, something that scared her. He moved his mouth over hers and she felt her name spoken with such a reverence tears burned the back of her eyes.

"I could not be in the same room and not want you."

She wanted the heady, fast passion of earlier, but Daniel had other ideas. He cupped her face as he continued to kiss her. She allowed her eyes to shut as he slowly deepened the kiss. It wasn't crazy as earlier, but this was much more dangerous. She was melting, literally melting. Her body, her mind, her body...her heart. She could not hold back from the simple kiss. It was impossible.

She could feel his manhood harden against her and her body respond on instinct. He rolled over, pulling her along, and she found herself atop him.

"Daniel, what are you doing?"

The smile he flashed was filled with masculine devilment. "We are going to try this a different way."

She looked down at him and her eyes widened. "Really?"

He nodded. "Lift up on your knees and take me inside of you."

She hesitated and then did as he said. It was a different

feeling. She was sore from earlier, but the amazing sensation of being connected to him this way helped her ignore the discomfort. It did not take her long to find her rhythm as she moved up and down, enjoyed being the one in control. He lifted up and took a nipple into his mouth, his expert tongue moving over the tip, then pulling it into his mouth.

Soon that familiar tension built within her. Her body tightened and, try as she might, she could not seem to get to that pinnacle. Daniel reached between their bodies and pushed her over into the free fall of release. Even as she was convulsing with it, he rolled them back over. He came to his knees and lifted her hips. He thrust in and out of her. Her body, just recovering from her last orgasm, was pushed into another. She shattered as he shouted her name again.

Anna watched Daniel pull his trousers up and sighed with regret. It really was a shame he could not come back to bed. She did not think she had enough of him in bed.

"I heard that," he said, amusement threading his voice. "I cannot chance anyone seeing me leave your room."

She pulled her knees up to her chest and wrapped her arms around her legs.

"I do not see the reason why. House parties are notorious for assignations."

He glanced at her. "Not for virgins with good reputations."

She shrugged, not caring much about her reputation. There was enough of her mother in her to know that she should care, but what had it gotten her? Nothing.

"Now," he said as he sat in the chair beside her bed and started to don his boots. "I will talk to your mother, but we will have to wait with a formal announcement until after I have spoken to Sebastian."

And just like that, the slow, easy feeling the night before

had given her vanished. Panic replaced it, her stomach muscles clenching in sudden tension.

"Why ever would you worry about them?"

Without looking up, he said, "I have to get their approval for our marriage."

For a moment, she held the words close to her heart. How many times had she dreamed of this, wished on the first star to hear those words come out of his mouth? She had wanted this more than anything else in the world.

"I did not agree to marry you."

He looked at her, his face unreadable. "What do you mean?"

"I mean that I never said I would marry you."

Irritation stole over his expression now. "What was last night about?"

"Do you marry every woman you take to bed?"

"Do not answer my question with a question. What did you think going to bed with me meant?"

She shrugged, hoping it looked more nonchalant than she felt. Inside, her heart was pounding, her stomach roiling. The one thing she had ever wanted was here for her. It was as if her fantasy and nightmare had been rolled into one big mess. He did not love her. He wanted her, maybe he needed her. But she knew one day he would leave her. He would grow bored and move on to find a paramour outside of their marriage. And she would die.

She shook her head, trying to show her confusion. "I thought that it was just a night of pleasure."

Anger leapt into his eyes, turning them a fascinating shade of red. From behind clenched teeth, he said, "I do not think for a moment you really thought that I would take my best friend's sister to bed without knowing the consequences."

A knife to the heart would have been less painful. She did not show the pain he had caused. She would deal with that later. Instead, she smiled.

"I do not wish to marry."

He settled his hands on his hips and frowned down at her. "That is absurd."

Irritation, anger and pain twisted inside of her, but she would not let him see that. She was never going to be vulnerable to a man again, especially this man who could hurt her so easily.

"No, it isn't. I have my money, my work...why ever would I need a husband?"

"What about the babe you could be carrying?"

She had to keep herself from touching her stomach, wishing it were true, but she shook her head.

"It isn't likely."

"How will you explain it if you are?"

"Then we can discuss marriage. But I see no reason to worry about it now, or chain ourselves to each other because of one night."

The scorching look he sent her would have burned a lesser woman. "If you think that I am not touching you again, you are insane."

The words sent a hot thrill racing through her. She had hoped he would not turn away from her. She knew there was a chance when she turned down his marriage proposal.

"So, we can carry on an affair." She smiled at him which seemed to make him even angrier than before.

"Just like that. An affair?"

She nodded, unable to speak past the lump in her throat.

"I do not think so."

Her heart sank. "You have had affairs before."

"With women who knew the score. They did not expect a marriage proposal in the morning."

"Neither did I."

He blinked. "You are telling me you let me take you to bed last night knowing we would not marry?"

"Yes."

She heard some shuffling in the hallway and knew he needed to leave. Granted, she did not care about her reputation, but she would not want it to reflect badly on her mother.

"You need to go."

"We are not finished with this discussion."

Before she could argue with him, he swooped down and gave her a quick, wet kiss. It was enough to curl her toes and have her heart beat out of control.

"I will accompany your carriage back today."

Her head was still spinning as he opened the door, stuck his head out to check the hallway. He stepped out, but poked his head back in. "I mean it, Anna. We are not done with this."

With that, he shut the door. She flopped back onto her pillows and closed her eyes. The scenes from the night before played through her head. Every touch, every sigh, every glorious moment. She held those memories close to her heart, and she would for the rest of her life. Just as she would if he kept his promise of taking her to bed again. It would not last, could not. Affairs rarely did, and she knew before long Daniel would end it. That she would deal with when it happened.

She would live in the moment for once in her life. No planning, no worries. She would not think of what was to become of her later, or how she would feel when Daniel took another woman as a lover.

But even as she promised herself that, she felt the tears streaming down her face. She had wanted to say yes to his proposal...to forget the one vow she had given herself years earlier. Marrying Daniel would be heaven and hell...and she would only hurt herself in the end. He did not love her. He wanted her for now, desired her in a way she had never expected from a man. She would be happy for a time, but the moment he took his first mistress, she would break. She would not let him know of her feelings, keep them locked away. She might not be as worldly or experienced as his former lovers, but she understood the way to conduct an affair. Messy feelings of love were not welcomed. And when it came time to part, it would happen without tears, without recriminations.

Now though, with the first light of the morning peeking through her drapery and the soft sounds of the house waking up, she turned her head into her pillow and cried.

Chapter Seventeen

Daniel stormed around his bedroom and ignored the interesting looks Jack kept tossing his way. He knew he was acting like an ass, but he didn't care. He had lived for thirty years without ever proposing to a woman. Now he had done it twice in less than three days and she had refused him...even after giving him her virginity. He thought she would jump into his arms with joy, thank him, let him love her again. Instead, she had refused his suit and then proposed they have an affair.

"I take it you did not get enough sleep last night?" Jack's sardonic tone grated on Daniel's already raw nerves.

He said nothing as he continued to pace his room. He had too much on his mind right now to be worried about one fickle woman who would take an affair over respectability. What was she thinking? There was no doubt in his mind the woman loved him, or at least cared for him. She would not have given herself to him the way she had the night before if she did not. He stopped in front of the window and stared blindingly out it, not taking in the activity below. Instead, his mind drifted back to the night before, the feel of her flesh against his, the way her sigh sounded in the dark, and the wonderful feeling of waking up beside her. He did not think he would ever be able to sleep without her by his side. He had no idea how he knew it, but he knew it to be true.

"I know you don't want to marry, my lord, but I think you

should just ask the chit and put yourself out of your misery."

He sighed. He knew that Jack meant well.

"I did."

Silence filled the room behind him, and he turned to find Jack staring at him. "She turned you down?"

Before he could answer him, there was a slight knock at the door. It definitely sounded female and he rushed to the door, his heart happy that Anna might have changed her mind. The moment he opened it and found Jo standing there, his smile faded.

"What do you want?"

She smiled and stepped over the threshold. "Good to see you this morning."

He poked his head out in the hallway to make sure no one had seen her come into his room, then shut the door.

"I take it you did not spend the night with your Lady Anna."

Agitation marched down his spine. His head was already starting to throb. "She is not my Lady Anna."

"She turned him down." The whispered comment came from Jack.

Joanna's eyes widened. "She turned you away from her bed? I am surprised."

"No, she did not do that. That she had no problem with. It was my proposal of marriage this morning that she flung back in my face."

Utter silence filled the room again and he had a sneaking suspicion that they were trying not to laugh at him.

"I am surprised," Joanna said.

"You are not the only one. When I told her I would talk to her mother and her brother—"

"You told her?" Joanna asked.

"Yes."

The laughter that bubbled up out of her had him narrowing his eyes.

"You told her? Daniel, I am assuming that she was a virgin and had never taken a man to bed."

He nodded, once.

"And the night after she accepts you, you told her you were going to marry her?"

"Yes, and she flung it back in my face. Said there was no reason to get married, that we could just have an affair. When I pointed out that our night together could result in a babe, she said we could wait and see."

And the pain of it still left his heart raw. It hurt him in places he did not know he possessed, and he hated it. Every bit of his control had vanished and he did not know if he would ever get it back.

"I would expect that much from her."

He cut Jo a nasty look and walked to the window again. He did not know what to do, where to look. The Viper was out there plotting his demise, probably had a man stalking Anna, and he was standing here contemplating why she would not marry him. It was foolish, but he couldn't seem to stop thinking about it.

"I will never understand her. When she came to town, the only thing she talked about was getting married."

"Oh, Daniel. The one woman you moon over and you keep messing it up. When are you going to learn she is not who you think she is? That girl that she was several years ago is no longer. This is a woman, one who has been hurt deeply. Dewhurst did not only take her pride, but I am sure he hurt her heart."

He glanced over his shoulder at his aunt. The rumors of their affair had worked well for them, allowing them to meet for work. But from the moment he'd met her years earlier, he had thought of her as his sister. There was a camaraderie there similar to what he felt for Sebastian. But at the moment, he wanted her to go away. He did not want to think about what that bastard had done to Anna, or that she might still be in love with him.

"It has been several years. She needs to get over it."

She laughed. "You are such a man. You told her you would marry her, and she should get over the humiliation and pain of what Dewhurst did to her."

"Yes." Although said like that, it sounded...wrong.

She glanced at Jack who bowed his head. "Gots to check on the horses."

After he slipped out of the room, she turned her attention to Daniel. "I do not think you understand just what Anna went through. She not only fell in love with another man, but could have caused her cousin's death."

He hated hearing that she had even contemplated love with another man. The ache inside his chest deepened. He knew for a fact she would have said yes to Dewhurst if he had asked for her hand at the time.

And that was the most painful cut of all. He had been a bounder, a user and a traitor and she would have married him.

"Daniel, did you ask her?"

He cut her a sharp glance.

"I did. I just told you I did."

"No, you told me that you told her."

"Of course I asked her. I didn't get down on bended knee or recite poetry, but I distinctly remember..."

It was then that he remembered he did not. He had argued, ordered and then left in so much anger that he did not realize the proposal he had planned had never materialized.

"Ah." She nodded in understanding. "And did you tell her

you love her?"

He refused to answer that, could not. He knew that he loved her, had for so long he could not remember when it started. It was different now, no so much an infatuation, but an obsession. A bone-deep understanding that she was the only one for him. Telling her was not acceptable. The moment he spoke the words out loud he would be at her mercy, and that was something he could not accept.

"I see that you did not." She sighed. "Take it from me, waiting to tell someone you love them can haunt you. Especially if you wait too long."

He knew she spoke of his uncle, a man most people would never describe as loveable, or even likeable, but Jo had loved him. Daniel had seen it whenever they were together.

"Just promise me you will not let what you do, what you feel you must do, keep you from finding happiness."

He nodded, not knowing what else to say. There was such sadness, such pain in her voice that it humbled him.

She drew in a deep breath, bringing herself back under control. "Now, I am here because I am not going to London. Simon has information about the poisoner, and I am going to meet up with him at the estate."

"Jo, you should not obsess."

"If it were Anna, what would you do?"

The thought of her being hurt was almost too much to bear. A flash of pain cut into his heart so deeply, the viciousness of it left him amazed.

"That is what I thought. Also, I want to talk to Simon about this Viper issue. He said he would talk to some of their old retainers. He thinks that it has to be someone in the ton."

Daniel wanted to refute that, but he mulled the idea over in his mind. It made sense. Only someone with access to the house party would know he was here. Oh, the servants did, but who else would be able to walk about unnoticed around the estate?

"Of course it is." Hadn't he even thought that earlier? "Why did I forget?"

"You are too close to it. He murdered your father so you have no objectivity."

"Not unlike you and this poisoner."

Her lips twisted into a wry smile. "Touché. I'll stop if you do."

"Not a chance."

"That is what I thought." She walked to him and gave him a quick bus on the cheek. "Make sure you tell her soon."

He nodded and she left him alone to his thoughts. It wasn't a new idea, but it was asinine he hadn't kept it in mind while he'd been at the house party. It had taken him long enough to come up with the theory. Of course, when it had happened, he had been lost in a river of grief, his own, his mother's, his sisters'. They were a close-knit family and losing his father had devastated all of them. He made a mental note to talk to his mother as soon as possible about the idea of who was close enough to kill his father.

With that idea tucked away, he turned his mind toward the problem of Anna. He knew he needed to tell Anna, but would she believe him? There was a chance she would, and there was a chance she would throw it back in his face. He knew men used the word to seduce, but he had never used it with a woman. He had been careful to keep himself separate, whole. With Anna, he had no choice.

Who was this woman he knew now? He knew he loved her. It was odd, because although she was not the woman she had been several years ago, he knew without a doubt he still loved her. Because beneath the new bravado, the self-reliant tenacity, lurked the girl he had known. She was kind to a fault and would do everything in her power to keep from hurting someone. Her beauty had only deepened over the last few years, giving curves to her slender form, leaving her breathtaking.

He would have to devise some plan to show her his love. If he told her, Daniel knew that she would not believe him, would think he was just using it to gain her acceptance. He could press, go to Sebastian, tell him what happened. His friend would insist on marriage, but he wasn't too sure that Anna would agree. In fact, he had a nasty feeling she would turn him down, even in the face of her brother's anger.

No, he would have to show her. He would go along with the idea of an affair and he would make sure that she accepted him and soon. If she resisted, he would somehow get her brother involved.

And if it didn't work, he might just kidnap her and make a dash for the Scottish border. Once in Gretna Green, she would have no choice in the matter. One way or another, Anna would be his wife.

Chapter Eighteen

Anna spent most of her time thinking about the situation on the way home. Daniel did accompany them, but the weather was rather nice for the time of year so he rode outside of the carriage. She knew there were things that Daniel would never tell her, could never tell her. Still, she felt there was more to this story than he was letting on. He kept doling out pieces of information as if she was too simpleminded to handle it all at once.

"What has you frowning, Anna?"

She looked up as her mother studied her.

"Do men always think they know everything?"

Her mother chuckled. "Indubitably."

Anna sighed. "That is what I was afraid of."

"Is there something you need to tell me?"

At first, panic pricked her heart, had her tummy doing somersaults. Had her mother realized she had slept with Daniel? Careful study told her that her mother had not figured it out—yet.

"No. It is just, I thought after all this time people would take me more seriously."

"Do you truly believe people do not? Why, I know that you are thought of highly with the society matrons for your work with the orphanage."

Anna shrugged. "It seems that most men do not take my intelligence seriously."

"Take it from me, most men don't."

"It is silly. Why, most of them can do no more than place bets in gaming halls. Why is hard work with the poor or such things any less?"

Her mother sighed. "Do you really want to tell me what is bothering you?"

Anna wanted to, wanted to tell her mother everything. About the night she had spent in Daniel's arms, the fact that someone was trying to kill him, that she might just be in love with the only man too dense to actually understand her.

Instead she shook her head. "No. I was just annoyed by some of Lord Seaton's comments last night."

"Lord Seaton is an idiot."

Anna laughed. "That he is. Do not worry, I would never marry him."

"Of course not. I don't want you to marry just to say that you are married. I want you to find someone to love."

She looked out the window and caught sight of Daniel riding a little away from their carriage. "That would be nice."

But she knew that it would not happen. He was not interested in love. Oh, making love he was ready for, but he would not ever admit love...because he did not. He would be like most of the men in the ton, happily married with a mistress on the side. He would never treat her badly, and he would be discreet. But she would know...and she would die a little inside each time he left her for someone else.

There was one thing she could do though. She needed to know more of his world, know just exactly what was going on. Daniel would just have to come to terms with the fact that she was definitely going to help.

"You want what?" Daniel asked as he started at Anna across the expanse of his study. It was enough that she had shown up unannounced. That had gotten his hopes up, made him think she might be bending in her refusal of his suit.

"I said I need to know more about this thing that you do."

"I have told you everything."

He told that lie easily. When you had been telling it for years, it was easy to do. Apparently, Anna was not satisfied. Her eyes narrowed. "I am not trying to pry, but I think I need to know exactly what is going on."

"And why would you?"

She frowned. "Because if I know what is happening around me, I might be more alert. You cannot expect me to stand idly by."

He had, and he knew he should not have. Anna had never been the type of person who would allow things to happen to her. Or she hadn't been. The last three years he had mistaken her good works and absence in society as a change in character.

"I told you everything I know."

"Who is this Viper person?"

"I told you."

"No, you said he was after you, trying to kill you. Now he was watching me. But who is he?"

From the militant look in her eyes, he knew she would not let it go. "Have a seat."

"You are not going to get me to change my mind."

"I would never dream of it. Please have a seat."

"I have a right to know. Especially since this man is—"

"Oh for the love of God, will you just sit down and shut up so I can tell you."

She snapped her mouth shut and did as he ordered. "I

want you to know that I do not like your tone."

He stared at her. "You are giving me lessons on comportment?"

"I find your manner rude."

"I find it odd that a woman who refused my suit after I took her virginity thinks she has the right to tell me how to behave."

Her chin came out as she crossed her arms beneath her breasts. He knew he was in for a fight.

"Now I will tell you what I know, which is next to nothing."

"But you said he killed your father?"

He nodded. "We never knew who it was. Father had begun receiving notes here and there, all signed by a man by the name of Viper."

"You are assuming it is a man."

"Well, of course it is a man."

"Women can kill. They have done so in the past."

He acknowledged that with a nod. "We know that this is a man. He was seen leaving the area."

"What did he look like?"

"The description was, in lack of a better word, nondescript. We realized later he probably disguised himself."

She nodded as she worried her bottom lip.

"We have tried for years to ferret out who it was. We were sure that he had died or left England until I got the letter."

"And he tried to kill you."

"No, he hired someone to kill me. We found him today."

"What did he say? Did he have a description?"

Daniel shook his head. "He was unable to give us any information."

Which was the truth. They had found a man who fit the description that Anna had given her driver floating in the

Thames this morning. But Daniel did not think he would tell her that.

"So you have no leads, have no idea who this man is. It must be driving you mad."

He smiled. "A bit. Not as much as someone else."

"Who? Is there another spy?"

He rolled his eyes. "No. I am talking about you."

"Oh." Her face flushed. It was the blush that did it, that drew him to her. He had been itching to touch her since she had walked into his study dressed in a blue walking dress, her cheeks pink from the cold weather outside. It was hard not to look at her and remember what lay beneath the fine fabric. He had been dreaming it for three days now, losing sleep and waking up aroused and grumpy. Seeing her in his house left him raw and needy.

He rose and walked around the front of the desk. He settled his hip on the edge.

"Was there anything else?"

She looked up at him. "Well, yes. You said you think the orphanage is safe? There was that break-in attempt a few weeks ago."

He shook his head. "I thought you said it was a working girl who wanted refuge."

"That was the first time. But she said there was a man hanging about. Sebastian told the guards, but since they didn't notice the first time…"

That bit of information he had not heard, but from the sincere look in her eyes, she had not been hiding it from him.

"Do not worry. I have a man on it all the time, and your brother still has the two guards. The orphanage is safe."

She smiled and settled against the back of the chair. "That is a relief."

He stood, pulled her up and out of the chair and into his arms. "Now that we have that taken care of—"

"Daniel."

"I think we need to have a little time to build this affair you want so badly."

Anna gasped as Daniel settled back into the chair behind his desk. The sound was more erotic than anything he had heard in a good long while.

"Really, Daniel, you cannot mean to..." She gestured with her hand.

"No, because knowing my luck, someone will knock and interrupt us. But I do want to have a few kisses."

Before she could say no, he swooped in to silence her with his mouth. He had meant to dally, tease. Instead, the moment he slipped his tongue into her mouth, he found his body responding, taking control. The scent of rosewater filled his senses. She was warm and round and his need for her had not dimmed even a little in the last three days since their return. If anything, it had grown, tripled. His every thought seemed to be about her, about having her here with him, taking her to his bed and keeping her there.

She slipped her hands over his shoulders and slanted her head to give him more access. Heat blasted through him, fast, furious, his cock throbbing in an immediate, painful erection. He had been half-aroused from the moment she walked into the study, but now, with her in his arms, his body was ready to conquer.

He needed to make sure she needed him as much as he needed her. The kiss went from sensual to downright carnal when she moved closer to him. He could feel her hardened nipples through their layers of fabric. He was helpless to resist touching.

As he slipped his hand to her breast, he knew he was lost.

In all his time he had never been so consumed, so entranced by a woman. The need to conquer, the primitive soul surfaced, the warrior who wanted nothing more than to slide between her thighs and take what he wanted. Before he progressed any further, Anna pulled back from the kiss. He growled and moved to take her mouth again, but she was not having it.

"No, Daniel, you will not distract me."

"I think I am doing a damned good job of it."

She struggled to get off his lap, wiggling her backside against his already straining erection. He took control of the situation by lifting her off his lap.

"I want to talk about this. I need to know everything concerning me in this mess."

"I told you all you need to know."

There was a beat of silence, then she lifted her chin and crossed her arms beneath her breasts. "Are you refusing my request?"

If he couldn't tell what she was feeling by the way she was looking at him, her chilly tone definitely would have enlightened him.

"I told you what you need to know."

"Indeed?"

Agitated with her, with the situation, with the fact that he had been without her for three days, he rose from the chair and started to pace. He was not accustomed to sharing things like this outside of the family. They rarely spoke of it unless there was high activity.

"There is nothing that a lady needs to know, just know that you will be well protected." He fairly bit out each word.

"Do you not think I would be better protected if I knew more? Or do you not trust me?"

"I trust no one really. And besides, ladies of the ton are not known for keeping secrets."

"I think—"

Frustration and panic tightened in his gut.

"I didn't ask what you thought. I told you that I do not share information like this with anyone. Just leave it alone and go along to your little orphanage."

When she said nothing more, he glanced over his shoulder at her. The moment he saw her stricken expression, he felt like a bastard.

"Anna, I'm—"

"Never mind, my lord." She moved around the desk and strode for the door.

"Anna."

She stopped at the door but did not turn to face him.

"I think we said enough to each other for now, do you not?"

He could hear the tears in her voice and felt even lower than before.

"I didn't mean to insult you."

She sniffed. "I know you didn't. And that is somehow worse."

Without another word, she left his study, shutting the door behind her with a quiet click. He took several steps toward the door, ready to follow her, to apologize, but he stopped. He knew that she would not believe him at the moment, and he knew without a doubt, she was not ready for an apology.

He thrust his hands through his hair and let out a frustrated growl. What the hell had happened? He had given her some information, not everything, not all of it. But he had told her what he thought she needed to know. He dropped his hands. He heard noise at the front of the house and went to watch her departure. As Jiggs handed her up into the carriage, he saw her offer a smile, but it wasn't the way she had looked just moments before his comments. This smile did not reach her eyes.

He cursed himself as he watched her carriage go by. Bloody hell, he had made a mess of things. What she didn't understand was that he rarely shared everything with everyone. Even his family. When he took over the job his father had controlled, the lying had begun.

He collapsed in his chair as the memories of his childhood came rushing back to him.

You mustn't tell anyone, Danny. Secrets are for family, and sometimes not even then.

How many times had he heard his father say that? Daniel had lost count. How did he share things with Anna when he didn't even know how? From the cradle to the grave, Bridgertons kept their secrets. They did not share, and even their closest friends were left in the dark.

There was a knock at the door.

"Go away."

But his visitor did not listen. The door crept open and Horace's round face popped through the opening. "Surely you have a moment for an old friend."

With a sigh, Daniel waved him in. He could not be rude to Horace, even if all he wanted to do was beat the living hell out of something, anything.

"Is there something you needed?"

"No, no. Just was stopping by on my way out. I had tea with your mother."

Daniel sat behind his desk and opened up his estate ledger. He said nothing as he pretended interest in the figures before him. His head was still pounding, his mind still trying to figure out how to solve his problem with Anna.

"I saw Lady Anna leaving. She did not look happy."

"We had a disagreement."

"Hmm, well, just be sure if you are planning on marrying the chit, that you get that fixed right away. And you shouldn't wait too long, dear boy. If you don't, they tend to find someone else."

He looked at Horace, a confirmed bachelor. "Is that what happened to you?"

He shook his head. "Sadly, no. The love of my life barely knew I was alive once she met the man she married."

"Ah."

"Now, I am an old fool, but I will give you some good advice. You need to make sure you understand the woman you love, know what makes her tick. If you had a fight, find something that will prove to her that you are sorry."

"That works?"

"Women are simple creatures." He sighed and lifted himself out of the chair. "Well, I must be moving along. I have some things to do before getting ready for the ball tonight."

He turned to leave, but Daniel could not help but ask, "Horace, is that why you never married? Surely there are other women out there."

The smile he offered Daniel was tinged with sadness and regret. "No. There are many women out there, but there is only one like your mother."

Stunned, Daniel watched him leave. When he was alone, he turned over the events. Horace was wrong. Women were not simple creatures. They were the most complex puzzle ever invented. He had done some major damage today, but he would figure out something to fix it.

Jack opened the door to Daniel's bedroom without knocking. Daniel was getting bloody sick of people just coming and going without any warning in his room.

He opened his mouth to say just that, but he snapped it shut when Simon followed him in.

"What the bloody hell are you two doing here this morning?" He looked at Simon. "I thought you were at your estate."

Simon grimaced. "I am worried a bit about Joanna, so I came into town."

"Her obsession?"

His younger cousin nodded. He was only a few years younger, his dark hair cut ruthlessly short. He looked his age until you looked at his eyes. The sapphire blue showed a world-weary understanding, one that Simon didn't have at the ripe old age of thirty-two.

"But I found something else out. I started doing a little research, and I think I might have pinpointed the Viper."

"Oh?"

"Well, recently, Lord Ashburn had been having some money issues. He has sold off everything he owned that wasn't entailed."

"I heard."

"A series of bad investments apparently left him running for the hills. But all of the sudden he seems to be a bit...more comfortable."

"What?"

"He's getting paid by someone," Jack said bluntly.

Ashburn was someone he did not know well. He was part of the older group, one of his father's contemporaries. He tended to host bacchanal-type parties at his estate. He'd married a merchant's daughter who'd died years ago. He had yet to remarry.

"He is the right age."

"Yes," Simon said. "I am not ready to condemn him. We

need to see what was going on all those years ago. See where he was. The man can never hold onto money to save his life, so he would be perfect to recruit."

The image of the older lord came to Daniel's mind. He was tall, his bulging belly and sagging jaws spoke of how he lived his life. The one thing that held him back was his intelligence.

"He isn't particularly bright."

Simon grimaced. "That is one thing that bothers me too. Unless someone in France is pulling the strings and he just follows the orders."

Daniel nodded. "Is that all?"

"No. I wanted to talk to you about Lady Anna."

Daniel stiffened, his irritation with their fight the day before coming back. He knew he had hurt her in some way, but he could not allow her involvement in the investigation. He had been horrible about it, but the fear he felt with her had him by the short hairs. Embarrassingly, she had no idea. She could command him to do anything but convince him that she should be involved in the investigation.

"What?"

Simon cast him a look at his sharp tone.

"Am I to understand that she is now a target because of you?"

He rolled his eyes. "She was in the area when I got stabbed. She was seen. Since then someone has been asking questions. And just when did you get to be in charge?"

"Since you became sloppy because you are in love with Lady Anna."

Anger surged.

"What the bloody hell are you talking about?"

Simon glanced at Jack. Jack shrugged.

"Daniel, you know being in your presence will cause her to

be a target. I have never seen you make a decision that put a civilian in harm's way. Besides, Jack said you are positively dotty over her."

The amusement he heard in his cousin's voice was salt to his wound.

"Did he?"

Jack grinned, apparently ignoring the lethal tone in Daniel's voice.

"Indeed. He said you ordered her to get married, but she refused you." The nasty smile Simon offered him told Daniel he was enjoying this a little too much.

"How do we get anything done with all of you gossiping like old women?"

Simon laughed, the sound a bit rusty, but it was good to hear. "By God, you *are* in love with her."

"How would you like to be forced to be in charge of our activities in Northern Scotland? The very tip of the Highlands."

Simon sobered. "You do need to be careful, Daniel. The one thing I do know is Ashburn is at his Yorkshire estate, but do not let your guard down."

He rolled his eyes again and looked at Jack. "When did I become the wet-behind-the-ears whelp?"

Simon smirked. "I would say it was about the time Lady Anna saved you. You were lost to us after that."

Chapter Nineteen

Daniel stood watching Anna read. It was mid-afternoon and quite warm for a spring day in London. She apparently took advantage of the day and came out to read. It was uncommon for him to find her alone like this now. He knew she was safe here in her family's gardens. So, watching her for a few minutes, he took in his fill.

She had always been a pretty girl. All those blond curls, brilliant blue eyes and her gregarious nature attracted everyone...children, adults, animals. She had grown into a beautiful woman who tempted him beyond his better judgment. But she was no longer so open. Knowing he had a part in that did not make his task easier.

He stepped forward and knew the moment she heard him approaching. She looked up, her gaze wide and her mouth curving into a welcoming smile. He hated watching her gaze go weary, her smile dim.

"Daniel. I had not expected to see you today."

Her voice was formal, stiff, and it made him angry. Knowing he had no one to blame but himself did not make it any easier. He said nothing until he seated himself next to her.

"I wanted to apologize."

That caught her attention. She studied him but said nothing.

He smoothed his hands down his trousers. "I... Well, I was a bit harsh yesterday."

One blond eyebrow rose. "Indeed?"

"I just cannot allow you to interfere."

If anything her back grew more rigid. "I think you made your position clear to me yesterday."

He sighed. "I just cannot bear it."

Her fingers ran over the cover of the book she had been reading. "I said you made yourself clear yesterday, Daniel. You do not need to drum home the idea that I have nothing to offer in the way of help."

He frowned. "That is not what I meant."

"Yes, you did. You said there was nothing of concern to me in your work."

"Agreed."

She said nothing for a long time, refusing to meet his gaze.

"Anna?"

"I..." She shook her head.

"What?" When she still didn't look at him, he slid his hand over hers. "Please, tell me."

Her shoulders slumped. "I know you do not think me very smart, but I did not think you thought that I had nothing to offer."

It was then that he realized he had been completely wrong. How had he not seen it before? Because, as Jo had told him, this woman was not the girl he knew. The depths in this woman, the amazing complexity of her emotions would take him a lifetime to figure out. How could he convince her he didn't mean that?

He slid his fingers beneath her chin and turned her to face him. "It isn't that I think you stupid, Anna. It is too dangerous for you."

She looked away. "I see."

"What exactly do you see?"

"You have no problem having Lady Joanna involved in all of your activities."

"That was not my choice. That was my uncle's decision."

She glanced at him. "You truly did not want me involved because you wanted to keep me safe?"

He nodded. "No one can call you stupid."

"I promise you it has been said more than once."

Anger whipped through him. "Tell me who had the audacity to call you stupid and I will throttle the bastard."

Her eyes widened. "Why on earth would you do that?"

She did not understand. That for every pain she went through, he felt it too. Looking at the confusion in her gaze, he knew she did not. Even now after what they had shared, she did not understand the depth of his feelings.

He opened his mouth to correct the mistake, but the sound of approaching feet stopped his words. Something drew Anna's attention over his shoulder and the smile that filled her expression clogged the air in his throat. He swallowed and forced himself to look at what had drawn her attention.

Colleen tried to catch her youngest as she ran laughing toward them. Millicent did not even pay any attention to him, but made a beeline for Anna. Anna laughed and pulled her up onto her lap.

"Hello, Millicent."

The little girl babbled.

"I am sorry. She heard your voice, Anna, and that was all it took," Colleen said with a smile.

"No worries." She kissed the cherub on the mouth and made her laugh.

"Daniel, I did not know you were here. Sebastian is actually at his club at the moment."

"Ah...yes, Templeton told me. I...ah, came out here to see...Anna."

Colleen's eyes danced. "Yes, I see that."

An uncomfortable silence filled the air among the adults, while Millicent babbled nonsensically. It was then he realized Colleen had no place to sit. He stood and she waved him back, but he shook his head.

"I have a meeting with my man of business."

He stood for a moment and then bowed. "I shall see you at the theater tonight."

Anna frowned. "The theater?"

"Oh, your mother said you and she would accompany my mother and me to the theater tonight."

She sighed. "Of course. She had not told me."

"Well, I will be off."

He bowed again and headed out. The chatter of the two women ensued, punctuated with happy giggles from Millicent. He looked over his shoulder and saw Anna lift Millicent in the air. A stream of babbling and giggling burst from the young girl. Anna pulled her back into her arms again and Daniel stopped, arrested by the sight. The two heads were together, one blonde, one strawberry blonde, their sounds of joy intermingling. The only thought that came to his mind was *mine*. He wanted that. He wanted Anna in his life, he wanted children and he wanted them with her.

There were things he had to do, namely find the Viper, then hand everything over to his cousin. As he strode through the garden, determination soared. He would have a life...because he just realized there was something worth living for.

Anna bit back a gasp the moment strong male fingers

slipped down her arm then tangle with hers. Without looking she knew it was Daniel. From the moment he entered the ballroom she had been nervous.

"I see that you are not dancing. Is there a reason?"

"We only just arrived." Which was true, but she had not felt like dancing. Except with him. But she was loath to admit it. It was bad enough she had been dreaming of him. She had awakened more than once in the last week with his name on her lips and her hands between her legs. She had never known what it was to need this way.

"I thought you might be waiting for me?" He said the words as flirtation, but there was something beneath it, something that had her looking sharply in his direction.

She said nothing and continued to watch the dancing. If any man approached, the look Daniel gave them discouraged any of them.

"Daniel, you must stop that. People will begin talking, and I think if we are to conduct an affair, we should not spend so much time in public together."

She did not look at him when she spoke, but she could feel his gaze.

"Indeed? Well, I will tell you this. While we are conducting this affair, you are not to dance any waltzes with anyone but me."

The possessive note in his voice should have irritated, and it did. Still, a part of her, the part that loved him, that wanted him with a need that had scared her more than once in the last couple of days, rejoiced.

"I think I can dance with whomever I want."

"Not if you want him to survive the night."

She gaped at him. "Are you threatening me?"

"No. Just any man who thinks he can touch you."

He said it in a tone that sounded more like regular chatting. "That is absurd."

"You refuse my suit, but you expect me to allow other men to touch you. I think not." He crossed his arms over his chest.

"You are being a boor."

When the music changed into a country reel, he pulled her behind a statue and then out a door. They stepped into a servant's hallway and then he tugged her down to another door. With an ease that had her gaping at him again, he slipped through the door, pulling her behind him.

"I am assuming your mother is otherwise engaged?"

She nodded. The darkened room must have been a library or study, definitely closed off from the party. He released her hand and went to another door. She heard the lock click shut. Nerves that had been shimmering were pulled tighter when she realized they were utterly alone, with no hope for escape.

"Why are we here?" Even as she asked it, she knew why.

"What do you think? You said you wanted an affair."

It had been four days since she had seen him. They had been to the theater and had not had a chance to be alone. Her mother had not wanted to go out, so she had taken the time to think things through.

"Yes."

He stepped behind her. The heat from his body warmed her back. The room seemed smaller, quieter. More dangerous. He skimmed his mouth over her bare shoulder.

"You wore this just to drive me insane, did you not?"

She should deny it, but she knew she would be lying. It was another creation made to drive men crazy. She had never worn it, but tonight she had hoped to see him. Hoped that he would see her.

"I did not know if I would see you." She tried to keep her

voice light, but he skimmed his teeth over her collar bone.

"Indeed?"

His tone told her he didn't believe her.

"It has been close to a week since I have seen you. I thought you might have changed your mind."

He paused, then continued on teasing her with his mouth. The low throb of arousal beat through her blood.

"There is no chance of that."

His voice had hardened, even as he moved his hands up her torso to her breasts. The moment he touched them, they ached. As if they knew his touch, knew he was the only one who could soothe the pain. She sighed the moment he pulled the fabric down and bared them to his hands. Expertly, he teased her nipples.

"I would rather spend more time, but with an affair, we do not always have a choice."

It seemed it did not matter. With just a touch, the sound of his voice, she was aching for him. Need clawed at her stomach. Wet heat flooded her body.

He sighed and his breath feathered out over her flesh, and she shivered. In the four days she had not seen him she had thought of him...and dreamed of him. More than once she had awakened, her skin damp, her body humming with need. She had ached between her legs, yearning for Daniel.

"I wanted to punish you, stay away longer." He nibbled on her earlobe. "But I could not do it. When my mother told me you were going to be here tonight, I had to come."

He spun her around and then, without any talking, scooped her up in his arms. As he walked to the couch, he kissed her. All the repressed need, desire, yearning she had felt in the last four days came back to her in that one kiss.

He still wanted her.

Her mind whirled. Her body rejoiced. She did not wait for an invitation but slid her tongue into his mouth. He jolted and she could not keep herself from celebrating that fact. He laid her on the couch and then followed her down. He kissed a path down her neck to her bosom, taking one needy nipple into his mouth. It shot a bolt of heat from her breasts down to her most private parts. She squirmed against him, needing relief. Dear Lord, he had barely touched her, but she was already straining against him, begging for him to take her.

He continued down her body, tossing up her skirts. The next instant he set his mouth against her stomach. All the tension gathered in her tummy then slipped lower. She shifted against him. He seemed to understand and moved lower. His tongue touched her first. It slipped inside, teasing her.

It did not take him long to push her up, to build the wonderful tension that she remembered and push her over into a free fall. But that apparently was not enough. He did it again, slipping his finger inside, his tongue touching the tiny bundle of nerves that rushed her headlong into another release. Every one of her nerve endings danced with delight, rejoicing in the pleasure he was offering.

It was then and only then that he moved back up her body. In the darkened room she could see the need etched on his face, the stark lines it created on his face.

"Who do you belong to?"

She wanted to deny it, say that no man would ever own her, but she could not. She shook her head, but it was of no use. He dipped his head and took her mouth in a wet, possessive kiss. She could taste herself there, the pungent flavor of her arousal, the desire he felt for her.

He pulled abruptly away and she tried to follow him, but he denied her.

"Who do you belong to?" he asked again.

This time, even though her mind rebelled against the idea, she said the words he needed, she needed, her heart and soul desired to hear.

"You, Danny. Only you."

With that, he plunged into her so forcefully that she came apart again. He thrust into her again and again. His fingers dug into her hips as he continued, pushed her further again, to reach the pinnacle but not allow her to shatter. It was only when he found his own that he shifted his position and pushed her over again. He was staring into her eyes. The intensity of his gaze scared her. She wanted to look away, but could not. This was not the patient lover. This was a man who had conquered her, the man she dreamt of each night, the one she yearned for during the day. This was her Danny, the man she had uncovered.

But even as she panicked, her body surrendered. She convulsed, drawing him deeper inside of her, and he groaned her name. He heaved a sigh filled with relief as he collapsed on top of her and nuzzled her neck. Moments passed and the only sounds in the library were their harsh breathing and the sounds of the staff drifting by. She felt herself drifting when Danny pulled back from her.

He leaned down once more to give her a quick, hard, thorough kiss. She wanted to object, to beg him to lie upon her. She loved to have his body press against hers.

But she said nothing as she watched him button his trousers. He shot her a wicked smile. "As long as you remember what you said, I will allow you to wear that dress."

All the warm feelings she'd had dissolved into anger. "And just what do you mean by that?"

He stilled and then braced his weight on the couch. He leaned his face down close to hers. "I do not like that dress. I do not like the way men look at you while you are in that dress. But as long as you promise that you are mine, I have no problem allowing you to wear it in public."

There was a hard edge to his words. She placed both hands on his chest and shoved. He moved back easily.

"I do not belong to any man."

There was silence. Then, "So, when we are making love, you do not mean what you say?"

She knew that her answer carried weight, knew that while she wanted to say that it didn't mean a thing, she could not. He might not love her, but she loved him. Lying to him just would not do.

"No. I do mean what I say, and in this, I do belong to you. But in my everyday life, I do not belong to you."

He said nothing, just continued to watch her in that patient way of his.

"I offered marriage."

How like a man. He had never asked for her hand in marriage, he had ordered. As if she was his chattel. "First, you did not. You told me we were marrying. Second, I do not ever want to belong to a man, not unless he fulfills one requirement."

She finished righting her clothing and then smiled brightly. "Now, how is this done? Do I go back alone?"

He said nothing but nodded.

She wanted to say something, but his expression sent a fresh wave of alarm rushing through her. There was something so stark, so forbidden in it she did not know what to say. Something cold unfurled inside of her, seeping into her blood, chilling her to the bone.

But she could not leave without one more touch. She rose to her tiptoes and brushed her mouth on his. "I will see you back in the ballroom."

He did not respond, to the kiss or the comment. She had a

feeling that she had done something wrong, said something, but she did not know what to do to fix it. She went to the door and unlocked it. She opened it, checked the hallway and found it clear.

"Anna." His voice was quiet, barely audible.

She turned, her hand still on the knob.

"What is the one thing you want?"

"What?"

"To marry. What is the one thing you want from a man?"

She did not answer at first. She did not know how to explain it, but she found the words that were the simplest.

"I need a man to love me for me."

He watched her as she stepped out into the hallway and closed the door. Her heart was aching as if she had lost something precious. She had known the relationship would not go on forever, but she felt that something had shifted tonight, something had changed. She worried her bottom lip as she walked down the hall. The sound of the ball grew louder, the voices, the music, the clinking of glasses. But she did not want to go in. She wanted to return to the library, to slip back into his arms...but that would not do.

She was so caught up in her thoughts that she did not see the man who approached her.

"Lady Anna?"

She looked up to find Lord Elwood smiling at her.

"Oh, I am sorry. I was lost in my thoughts."

"No worries. I was actually looking for you."

She smiled. "Was my mother looking for me?"

"No." He wrapped a hand around her upper arm, his fingers digging into her flesh. She glanced up and found the usually quiet, sweet eyes filled with sinister intent.

"I have been trying to get you alone since you thwarted my assassin in the alley that night."

Chapter Twenty

Daniel shoved a hand through his hair, his mind on the woman who had just left him. He should have known Anna wouldn't ask for anything halfway. He closed his eyes, her words playing over in his head. The woman would not give an inch, he knew that. Of course, he probably would not love her if she was a pushover.

What could he do? He wanted her, needed her in a way that he did not understand before tonight. Making love to her brought some primal beast out in him. He opened his eyes and stared at the closed door. It had taken all of his monumental control to allow her to walk out that door. Every instinct he had had screamed for him to grab her and pull her back in the room. Away from prying eyes and lusting men. But he did not have that right, and according to Anna, he would not unless he proved in some way that he loved her.

He wanted to sit in the darkened room and brood. But he did not have that luxury. He had to get back out into the ballroom and watch over Anna. He stepped out of the room into the hallway and only made it a few steps before Lady Victoria came rushing toward him. Worry etched her features and curdled his stomach. He did not want to be discovered before he had Anna's agreement of marriage.

"Have you seen Anna?"

"No. Why would I have seen her?"

"Oh, goodness, I do not have time for this. Dear boy, you slipped her out of the room over forty minutes ago through that hidden panel. I have a feeling you were not discussing politics."

He opened his mouth but she did not let him talk.

"I thought she was with you and I was worried that others had noticed. When I headed back this way, I only found this."

She raised Anna's dance card. Now panic swept through him. A missing dance card was one thing, Anna not making it back to the ballroom was another.

"Did you check the retiring room?"

She nodded. "I went there first. Then I found this down the hall."

He needed to think, needed to come up with some explanation. He had thought Ashburn was at his Yorkshire estate, far from Anna. He had let his guard down and put her in danger. He should have known better. This was a man who had been making a mockery of the War Department for years.

He held out his arm. "Let's get back to the ballroom, see if my mother knows anything."

"If you got her mixed up in this spy business, I will never forgive you. I swear Daniel, I was hoping for a wedding, but if she is hurt in any way, it will be a beheading."

He stopped and looked at her. "How did you know?"

She rolled her eyes. "Your mother told me years ago. We do not have time to go through all that now. Oh, there is Adelaide."

His mother walked sedately toward them, a serene look on her face, but he saw a glimpse of worry in her eyes.

"I have not found her. Any luck?"

Both of them shook their heads. Just then he caught a glimpse of Jack in the hallway arguing with one of the staff. He strode over and dismissed the servant.

"What did you find?"

Before he could answer, his cousin walked up behind him. His hair was a mess, his clothes not much better.

"I wanted to let you know what I found out. Jack here beat me to the door though." He tossed a nasty look at the old retainer. "Lord Ashburn wasn't the spy. He apparently was out of the country at the time of your father's death."

"But the money, the accounts..."

"All handled by his man of business, who also works for Lord Horace Elwood."

The gravity of his words shook Daniel to his core. The man who had been his father's best friend, who had stepped in and helped Daniel as he'd tried to take over the reins of an earldom. The same man who showed disdain for Anna on more than one occasion. Cold seeped into his blood.

"He's a family friend."

"Yes. And apparently he became a family friend for a reason."

"And he just left with Lady Anna."

His head whipped around at a breathless Jack. "What the bloody hell are you talking about?"

"I didn't know this latest bit of news, and I saw the two of them leave in his carriage."

"Dammit." He ran down the hall and out the front door, ignoring the footmen. Simon was running next to him, Jack pulling behind them.

"Daniel!" his mother yelled. "What has happened?"

He looked up at the woman he loved, the woman who had been the one person he could always count on, and realized that the news would break her heart. To know that a family friend, her husband's best friend, was his killer would surely cause her undue pain. But he had no time now to explain, to soothe. Knowing the Viper as he did, Daniel knew Anna was being held to trap him. .If he didn't act fast, the Viper would discard her without a thought.

"Don't worry. I know where she is. Tell Victoria I will bring her back safely."

After telling the driver where to go, he jumped into his cousin's carriage and joined both his cousin and Jack.

"Do you know where to go?" Simon asked.

His memory went back to the conversation that he had not picked up on, the details that he should have heard had he not been so wrapped in his pursuit of Anna. The one place she would hurt the most if it was destroyed.

"Oh, yes, I do know where to go."

"He will not come after me, you know." Anna tried to sound brave, but being tied up to a chair, staring at a man who kept mumbling to himself had her worried. She knew his plan was to draw Daniel here, but she knew he wasn't completely sane at the moment.

"Of course he will. You are the only thing that would get him to react. That or his family."

She tried not to show her reaction on her face. She knew no matter what, Daniel would pursue this, and as clever as he was, he would realize the one place Elwood would take her to was her orphanage.

"You were the one in the alley, the night Carlotta came to the orphanage."

He smiled. It was all teeth and no warmth. "People rarely pay attention to a little old man."

When Anna had realized the moment he planned to take her to the orphanage, she had fought him. Only the threat of killing anyone who tried to help her kept her quiet. She tossed another look of apology at Mrs. Markham, although she could not see it. He had hit the elderly woman over the head with the butt of his gun and she had been out since then. Anna needed to convince the man that she was not someone Daniel would risk his life for.

"I am just a family friend."

He cackled and she winced. His horrible laugh echoed through the vacant halls. She was worried one of the boys would come to the office in search of Mrs. Markham.

One eyebrow rose as his eyes focused on her. "Indeed? Is that why he spent the night in your room at the house party? Or maybe that is why you spent so long secluded in a locked library?"

She sniffed and tried to look indignant. "I have no idea what you are talking about. Even if it were true, he would not be dense enough to fall for such a stupid plan."

"I have to disagree with you, Anna," Daniel said from the entrance. "There is no way I could leave you at the mercy of this bastard."

She watched in horror as Lord Elwood turned the gun in the direction of Daniel.

"I knew you would come. You have proved harder to kill than your father."

Daniel never responded to that, but she saw the twitch in the corner of his eye. Facing his father's killer was bad enough, but knowing that this man, the one he had always looked up to, had killed him was a little much for anyone to bear.

"Why?"

"Why what, dear boy." His pleasant tone had her blood turning to ice.

"Why did you kill him? Why are you a traitor?"

Elwood shrugged. "You do not know what it is like."

"Explain."

He did not seem to like Daniel's tone of voice. Elwood apparently did not like to be ordered about by anyone, especially a younger man.

"Your father was the golden boy. You know that, don't you? He had all the money, all the friends. I thought myself so lucky when he took me under his wing at Eton. But then he made a mistake when we met Adelaide."

"My mother. What does my mother have to do with it?"

"She was all I ever wanted, ever needed. I had thought your father never meant to marry. I could not since I did not have my inheritance. Even after my father died, I had no money. Then your father stole her. She was dazzled by his money, by his position. She ignored me, tossed me aside."

His voice rose with every word. Daniel was trying his best to control his temper, his need to kill the man before him, but she knew he was doing his best not to cause either of them injury. As they continued to talk, she slowly rose from the chair.

"You never had a chance with her."

Elwood's face mottled with rage. "No. But then I had other things to worry about. My father could not control his urges, sank us into debt. I was one step away from debtor's prison when I was offered an opportunity of a lifetime."

"To kill my father."

A frown moved over his face. "No. I did not know of your father's stupidity until later. Much later. And you know the best of it? He told me."

His gleeful laugh sent a chill slipping over Anna's flesh and down her spine. There was an edge of insanity seeping into his voice, into his expression. She had seen a woman like this one time in White Chapel and she had been warned by locals to stay away.

"I wanted to laugh in his damned face when he revealed what he did, that he regretted you would have to take up the job. He wanted you not to become a spy, did you know that?"

There was a flash of pain in Daniel's eyes, one she was sure Elwood saw, one that he probably rejoiced in. If she could ever get out of here, she would make the man pay for that.

"No, I see he never talked to you about it. He wanted you to have a normal life. And while trying to come up with a way to disentangle his family from the spy network, he told me, asked my advice. And I knew then, knew I would have him. I would raise myself up to my superiors, and I would get rid of my nemesis."

"And through the years, the times you have come to our assistance, the time you spent with my mother, with me, walking my sister down the aisle...they were all as a traitor, spying on us?"

He shook his head. "No. That was genuine, but try as I might, your mother would never let go of that memory. Never allow herself to love again. Even from death, Edward is haunting me."

"And me? You knew for years I was a spy?"

"No. I really believed that you had decided not to do it, that your mother had made sure that you did not get involved. But imagine my surprise when I found out that you not only stayed in the game, but took over his position."

Anna edged toward the door unnoticed. Lord Elwood was ignoring her now, his gun centered on Daniel. If she could get out into the hallway, she could run for help. She knew her way around White Chapel even in the dead of night.

Hope sprang in her heart until Daniel flicked her a warning glance. It was enough to gain Lord Elwood's attention.

"Where do you think you are going, Lady Anna? I cannot allow you to leave. Not when I have such plans for you."

"You will not touch her," Daniel growled the command, his hands fisted at his sides.

The older man laughed. "As if you have any means to stop

me."

Daniel stepped forward, his stance threatening.

There was a sound at the door and the gun wavered in that direction. The door burst in at the same time that Daniel lunged. The gun went off, but Anna could not see what was happening. A man tackled her to the ground. She kicked and screamed, trying to buck him off of her.

There was another shot, then silence, except for her struggles. "Anna, it is Simon, Daniel's cousin."

She calmed then and looked up and saw the young man. He released her and she looked over to find Lord Elwood lying on the ground, blood pooling around him. Relief moved through her as she shoved Daniel's cousin away and rose to run to him. He was rising to his feet when she jumped him. He grunted when she hit him, but his arms closed around her.

"Oh, Danny, I am so happy you are okay. I was so worried."

She felt his mouth brush her temple and she pulled away. Tears blurred her vision as the night's events began to come to a realization.

It was then she saw the blood on his shoulder and the ashen color of his face. Her heart nearly stopped as terror screamed through her entire body.

"Jack! He's been shot."

Chapter Twenty-One

A sharp pain lanced through his shoulder as he was jostled about on the way to the carriage.

"Please be careful with him."

He knew without a doubt that Jack and Simon were trying not to laugh. He wasn't that badly hurt. It was just a flesh wound. But Anna had refused to allow him to walk. Once he was settled on the seat, Anna shoved Jack aside and joined him. She leaned forward, her gaze on his wound as she tended it. The scent of her, the warmth of her body, surrounded him, left him feeling a bit lightheaded.

"What were you thinking showing up there like that?" she asked.

"Trying to save your life. Which I point out, that I did."

"Humpf."

Apparently satisfied with what she saw, she sat beside him as Jack and Simon joined them.

"You know, you could thank me."

She said nothing. Anger vibrated off her in waves. He knew she was angry with him, mad that he had shown up at all. But dammit, what did she expect him to do? Allow a madman to kill her?

"Anna?"

"Thank you."

"That is all?" He could not keep the amusement out of his voice.

"What do you want, a lock of my hair?" Her voice quivered, telling him that she was not as calm as she seemed.

"Your hand in marriage will do." He could hear his words slur, his mind beginning to grow numb.

"Anna?" he asked, his head now growing fuzzy.

She cast him a wary glance and alarm spread over her features. "Okay, yes, I will marry you."

He grabbed her hand. "By special license. I do not want to wait."

She patted his hand. "I said I would, Daniel."

"I will hold you to it."

"I am sure you will. Not that you will remember."

He thought he heard Jack chuckle as he clutched Anna's small hand in his. His world faded into nothingness except for one thought—Anna would be his for a lifetime.

Two days later, Anna walked into his study, a smile lightening her face. She had been in and out of their house during that time, directing everyone—even his mother—to his care. He had been careful not to mention his proposal and her acceptance until he had everything in order. He knew she was convinced he had forgotten the whole incident, but he had not. He was going to hold her to her promise.

"Good morning, Daniel."

He would never get used to hearing his name on her lips. The way her pleasant voice rolled over the syllables, but he particularly liked it when she called him Danny.

"Good morning, Anna."

"Your mother said you had something to say to me?"

He motioned with his hand. "Come here."

Wariness crept into her expression and she glanced toward the door.

"Oh, I am not sure—"

"Higgens?"

His formidable butler stepped into the doorway.

"Yes, my lord."

"Shut the door."

"Yes, my lord."

Once it was closed, he motioned with his hand again. She hesitated long enough to irritate him. The woman just would not give him an inch.

"Anna." He could not, would not stop the growl that vibrated in his voice.

She obeyed then and stepped around the desk. Without any warning, he grabbed her hand and pulled her into his lap. She gasped and then laughed when he took a quick, hard kiss.

"I like the sound of that. You have not laughed much the last few days."

She looked at him, the shadows of the memories from that night darkening her expression. "I am so sorry you were shot. I know that if it had not been for me, you would not have been hurt."

He shook his head and knew that guilt was one of the reasons she had been a bit down. "I am the master spy, Anna. I should have suspected the man. He did come into his money quite suddenly, but no one really paid attention to him."

She cupped his cheek. "That is why he made a very good spy."

He nodded. "And one of the reasons I am giving it up."

Her eyes widened. "But you said it was a family business."

"My cousin is happy enough handling it for now. I have other more important things to accomplish now."

She cleared her throat. "Indeed?"

He nodded, trying not to smile. The woman was as transparent as water to him. He knew she loved him, knew that if she had a chance, she would have jumped in front of that gun the other night. Even as the thought made his blood run cold, he rejoiced in her actions. It proved she loved him even if she had never said the words.

"What would that be?"

"Planning our wedding."

Silence greeted him as she frowned.

"You do remember saying you would marry me, do you not?"

She patted his hand. "Daniel, seriously, I said it just to appease you."

"You still said yes. I have two witnesses."

She tried to get up from his lap, but he held onto her firmly.

"This is ridiculous!" She raised her arms up, almost hitting him in the face with her hand. "You do not really want to marry me and I will remind you, I did have one requirement."

"Let me see," he said, leaning back in his chair as if pondering the question. "What was it? Oh, yes, love. But I do love you, Anna."

"Do not make fun of me, Daniel. It would break my heart." The pain that tinged her voice almost broke his heart. He would do everything in his power that she never doubt his love ever again.

"But I do love you."

She sniffed as tears filled her eyes. "You think you do, or you feel obligated to say it because you took my virginity."

"No, I truly love you."

"You do not." Now she crossed her arms over her chest. He

was damned with difficult women in his life. His sisters, his mother, Jo and now the woman he loved, the one who he would walk over hot coals for, the one who claimed he did not love her.

"Why do you think I do not love you?"

She sighed. "When I came to town, you were horrible to me."

He leaned back in the chair and closed his eyes. He should have known his behavior over the years would come back to haunt him.

"Do you want to know why I acted that way?"

She glanced at him out of the corner of her eye, then fixed her gaze on her hands in her lap and nodded.

"You had always been My Lady Poppet. I remember Sebastian telling me you were coming to town, that you would be coming out. In my mind, I did not see you as a woman. I expected the girl I knew to appear. Instead, you were there."

"I do not understand."

She was still looking at her hands. He slipped his fingers beneath her chin. Unshed tears simmered in her eyes.

"I had thought never to marry. When you came to town, I regretted that decision. I wanted you from the moment of your coming out ball." Her eyes widened. "Worse, you were my best friend's little sister. Lusting after you was crossing a line. You were not a widow to be dallied with, and I did not want to put you in harm's way. After seeing what my father's death did to my mother, I did not want to put you through that. I acted the way I did because I wanted you more than I wanted my next breath. It physically hurt to see you with other men."

He reached forward and pulled out a piece of paper.

"I am not sure if you believe me, but I think this proves anything you need to know."

She stared at the piece of paper. "A receipt? For...Danny, this is a lot of money for the orphanage."

He smiled. "I wanted to buy you the most beautiful ring, but you are not an ordinary woman. I am sure that many women would love an engagement ring from me. Seeing how we will not be engaged for long, I did not see the reason. Besides, I assumed this would prove my point much faster than a silly ring."

She looked up from the paper, tears spilling down her face. "Oh, Danny."

"I love you, Anna. Not for your beauty, although there is plenty of that. No, I love that you are irritated with me right now, that you give your time to help those children, and I also love the fact that you probably have more courage than a woman should have. You are too intelligent for your own good. And I particularly love the way you call me Danny."

"Truly?"

He nodded. "So, will you marry me, love me?"

Tears of happiness streamed down her face. "Oh, Daniel, I have loved you for so very long." She hugged him then. "Yes. Yes, I will marry you."

"Now that is cleared up, I have gone two days without touching you and it has been driving me insane."

She giggled and tried to bat his hands away.

"Danny, we can't. You are not well enough, and besides the door isn't locked."

"Higgens."

The door opened slightly. "Yes, my lord."

"Shut the door and lock it."

"Yes, my lord."

Knowing his order would be obeyed, he smiled at Anna. "I assure you, I am well enough for certain activities."

The mischievous light in her eyes, the way her lips curved in invitation, was all he needed. His blood heated, his heart expanding with the love he saw there in her gaze.

"I do love you, Anna."

"Show me, Danny."

He smiled as he moved his mouth over hers, her sigh of pleasure filling the air as the bright sun lightened the room. She was his. Forever.

About the Author

Born to an Air Force family at an Army hospital, Melissa has always been a little bit screwy. She was further warped by her years of watching Monty Python and her strange family. Her love of romance novels developed after accidentally picking up a Linda Howard book. Since her first release in 2004, Melissa has had close to 30 short stories, novellas and novels released with seven different publishers in a variety of genres and time periods. Those releases included an Eppie nomination and two CAPA nominations, along with a multitude of best sellers. Her contemporary, *A Little Harmless Sex,* became an international best seller in June of 2005 and was named one of the 100 best selling Nookbooks of 2010.

Since she was a military brat, she vowed never to marry military. Alas, Fate always has her way with mortals. Her husband is an Air Force major, and together they have their own military brats, two girls, an adopted dog daughter and they live wherever the military sticks them. Which until recently always involved heat and bugs only seen on the Animal Discovery Channel. In her spare time, she reads, complains about bugs, travels, cooks, reads some more, and tries to convince her family that she truly is a delicate genius. She has yet to achieve her last goal.

If you want to know more about Melissa, stop by the following websites: www.melissaschroeder.net, http://groups.yahoo.com/group/Melsbookchatters/, http://twitter.com/melschroeder, www.facebook.com/pages/Melissa-Schroeder/17997114885. For all things Harmless, join the Facebook group www.facebook.com/group.php?gid=160200550663144&ref=mf.

She loves to hear from her readers so be sure to drop Melissa a note: Melissa@melissaschroeder.net or PO Box 2706, Manassas, VA 20108.

It's all about the story...

Romance

HORROR

www.samhainpublishing.com

Lightning Source UK Ltd.
Milton Keynes UK
UKOW052354030212

186634UK00001B/39/P